William Shakespeare's Twelfth Night: A Retelling in Prose

David Bruce

Published by David Bruce, 2022.

WILLIAM SHAKESPEARE'S TWELFTH NIGHT: A RETELLING IN PROSE

First edition. July 29, 2022.

Copyright © 2022 David Bruce.

ISBN: 979-8201910501

Written by David Bruce.

Table of Contents

Dedication

Dedicated to Carl Eugene Bruce and Josephine Saturday Bruce

My father, Carl Eugene Bruce, died on 24 October 2013. He used to work for Ohio Power, and at one time, his job was to shut off the electricity of people who had not paid their bills. He sometimes would find a home with an impoverished mother and some children. Instead of shutting off their electricity, he would tell the mother that she needed to pay her bill or soon her electricity would be shut off. He would write on a form that no one was home when he stopped by because if no one was home he did not have to shut off their electricity.

The best good deed that anyone ever did for my father occurred after a storm that knocked down many power lines. He and other linemen worked long hours and got wet and cold. Their feet were freezing because water got into their boots and soaked their socks. Fortunately, a kind woman gave my father and the other linemen dry socks to wear.

My mother, Josephine Saturday Bruce, died on 14 June 2003. She used to work at a store that sold clothing. One day, an impoverished mother with a baby clothed in rags walked into the store and started shoplifting in an interesting way: The mother took the rags off her baby and dressed the infant in new clothing. My mother knew that this mother could not afford to buy the clothing, but she helped the mother dress her baby and then she watched as the mother walked out of the store without paying.

***

The doing of good deeds is important. As a free person, you can choose to live your life as a good person or as a bad person. To be a good person, do good deeds. To be a bad person, do bad deeds. If you do good deeds, you will become good. If you do bad deeds, you will become bad. To become the person you want to be, act as if you already are that kind of person. Each of us chooses what kind of person we will become. To become a good person, do the things a good person does. To become a bad person, do the things a bad person does. The opportunity to take action to become the kind of person you want to be is yours.

Human beings have free will. According to the Babylonian Niddah 16b, whenever a baby is to be conceived, the Lailah (angel in charge of contraception) takes the drop of semen that will result in the conception and asks God, "Sovereign of the Universe, what is going to be the fate of this drop? Will it develop into a robust or into a weak person? An intelligent or a stupid person? A wealthy or a poor person?" The Lailah asks all these questions, but it does not ask, "Will it develop into a righteous or a wicked person?" The answer to that question lies in the decisions to be freely made by the human being that is the result of the conception.

A Buddhist monk visiting a class wrote this on the chalkboard: "EVERYONE WANTS TO SAVE THE WORLD, BUT NO ONE WANTS TO HELP MOM DO THE DISHES." The students laughed, but the monk then said, "Statistically, it's highly unlikely that any of you will ever have the opportunity to run into a burning orphanage and rescue an infant. But, in the smallest gesture of kindness — a warm smile, holding the door for the person behind you, shoveling the driveway of the elderly person next door — you have committed an act of immeasurable profundity, because to each of us, our life is our universe."

In her book titled *I Have Chosen to Stay and Fight*, comedian Margaret Cho writes, "I believe that we get complimentary snack-size portions of the afterlife, and we all receive them in a different way." For Ms. Cho, many of her snack-size portions of the afterlife come in hip hop music. Other people get different snack-size portions of the afterlife, and we all must be on the lookout for them when they come our way. And perhaps doing good deeds and experiencing good deeds are snack-size portions of the afterlife.

The Zen master Gisan was taking a bath. The water was too hot, so he asked a student to add some cold water to the bath. The student brought a bucket of cold water, added some cold water to the bath, and then threw the rest of the water on a rocky path. Gisan scolded the student: "Everything can be used. Why did you waste the rest of the water by pouring it on the path? There are some plants nearby which could have used the water. What right do you have to waste even a drop of water?" The student became enlightened and changed his name to Tekisui, which means "Drop of Water."

Cover Photograph for William Shakespeare's *Twelfth Night*: A Retelling in Prose:

https://pixabay.com/photos/girl-woman-beauty-portrait-reverie-5266760/

***

In this retelling, as in all my retellings, I have tried to make the work of literature accessible to modern readers who may lack the knowledge about mythology, religion, and history that the literary work's contemporary audience had.

Do you know a language other than English? If you do, I give you permission to translate this book, copyright your translation, publish or self-publish it, and keep all the royalties for yourself. (Do give me credit, of course, for the original retelling.)

I would like to see my retellings of classic literature used in schools, so I give permission to the country of Finland (and all other countries) to buy one copy of this eBook and give copies to all students forever. I also give permission to the state of Texas (and all other states) to buy one copy of this eBook and give copies to all students forever. I also give permission to all teachers to buy one copy of this eBook and give copies to all students forever.

Teachers need not actually teach my retellings. Teachers are welcome to give students copies of my eBooks as background material. For example, if they are teaching Homer's *Iliad* and *Odyssey*, teachers are welcome to give students copies of my *Virgil's* Aeneid: *A Retelling in Prose* and tell students, "Here's another ancient epic you may want to read in your spare time."

PREFACE

In Shakespeare's time, Twelfth Night was the night before Twelfth Day, the final day of the twelve days of Christmas. The First Day of Christmas is December 25, Christmas Day, and so Twelfth Day is January 5, which is the eve of Epiphany: January 6. According to tradition, Jesus was born on December 25, and the Visit of the Magi — the Three Wise Men from the East visiting the newly born Jesus and giving him gifts of gold, frankincense, and myrrh — occurred on January 6. Twelfth Night is a festive time and is full of merry-making and the playing of practical jokes. As you would expect, Shakespeare's *Twelfth Night* is a comedy.

CAST OF CHARACTERS

Main Male Characters

ORSINO, Duke of Illyria.

SEBASTIAN, Brother to Viola.

ANTONIO, a Sea Captain, Friend to Sebastian.

A Sea Captain, Friend to Viola.

VALENTINE & CURIO: Gentlemen attending on the Duke.

SIR TOBY BELCH, Uncle to Olivia.

SIR ANDREW AGUECHEEK.

MALVOLIO, Steward to Olivia.

FABIAN, Servant to Olivia.

FESTE, a Clown: Servant to Olivia.

Main Female Characters

OLIVIA, a rich Countess.

VIOLA, in love with the Duke.

MARIA, Olivia's Serving-woman.

Other Characters

Lords, Priests, Sailors, Officers, Musicians, and other Attendants.

CHAPTER 1

— 1.1 —

Duke Orsino, his attendant Curio, and some lords were in the Duke's palace in Illyria, which is located northwest of Greece. Musicians were playing.

Orsino said, "If music be the food of love, play on. Continue to play music until I grow sick of music, so that, having suffered from an excess, my appetite for love will sicken and then die."

He paused to listen to the music and then said, "Play that melody again! It has a languishing descent that sounded so sad. It passed over my ears like the sweet sound made by a gentle breeze that breathes upon a bed of violets and takes the scent of violets and carries it afar. That's enough. No more of that melody. It is not as sweet now as it was before."

He added, "Spirit of love, how lively and refreshing are you. Your capacity for receiving passions is as enormous as the sea's capacity for receiving tributary streams, yet everything that enters into you, of whatever strength and from whatever height, falls into diminishing value and a low price, even within a minute. Love is so full of constantly changing images that it alone is supremely imaginative and nothing can compare to it. Love can be strange. I am in love, and yet I want to be out of love. I wanted to listen to music, and then I did not want to listen to music."

An impartial observer could very well think, *The one thing Orsino, the Duke of Illyria, does love consistently is the idea of love itself. He is more in love with the idea of love than he is in love with the Countess Olivia, whom he says he loves. This is why he wanted to hear this love song.*

Duke Orsino's attendant Curio did not take Orsino's lovesickness seriously. He asked, "Will you go hunting, sir?"

"Hunting what, Curio?"

"The hart: a stag."

"Why, yes, I do go hunting," Orsino replied. "I go hunting for a heart, the noblest that I have: my own. When my eyes did first see Olivia, I thought that she purged the air of pestilence and plague! In that instant, I was turned into a hart like Actaeon was when he did first see Diana. Diana, a virgin goddess, was bathing naked and was not happy to be seen. To punish Actaeon, she turned him into a hart, and his hunting dogs pursued him and tore him into pieces. Ever since I saw Olivia, my desire for her pursues me and hunts me like savage and cruel hounds."

Valentine, another of Orsino's attendants, entered the room. Orsino had sent him to tell Olivia of Orsino's love for her.

Orsino said to him, "What news have you brought me about Olivia?"

"Sir, she would not admit me into her home and let me talk to her. But I do bring you the message that I received from Maria, her personal servant: 'For the next seven years, Olivia will not display her face to the open air. It shall always be veiled. She will be like a nun cloistered from the world. Once a day, her salt tears will water her chamber. The salt in her tears will season and keep fresh her love for her dead brother, whom she wishes to remember clearly and forever."

Orsino said, "Olivia has a sensitive heart because she will pay this debt of love to someone who was only a brother — someone she is related to by birth. She will love even more when Cupid's golden arrow — the arrow that causes people to fall in love — hits her and she loves only me, forgetting all her other loves. When that happens, her mind and heart and soul will be given to one person, and she will take a husband. Now I will go to my garden and see sweet beds of flowers. Love-thoughts lie rich when canopied with bowers. A shady and flowery garden is a good place to think about love."

— 1.2 —

On the shore of the Adriatic Sea on the coast of Illyria, the noblewoman Viola, as well as a sea captain and some sailors, had just landed after surviving a storm at sea that had sunk their ship.

Viola asked, "What country, friends, is this?"

The captain replied, "This is Illyria, lady."

Viola said, "I wonder what I should do now. My twin brother has almost certainly drowned and is in Elysium, the good part of the afterworld. But perhaps my brother did not drown. What do you think, sailors?"

The captain replied, "It is only by great good fortune that you yourself did not drown."

"And since I was saved, perhaps my poor brother was also saved."

"True, madam," the captain said. "Here is some comfort for you. I can assure you that when our ship split in two and sank and you and the few others here who survived held onto our drifting ship, I saw your brother acting bravely and resourcefully during such a dangerous time. He tied himself to a floating mast. I saw him keeping himself from drowning for as long as I could see him. He rode on the mast like Arion rode on the dolphin that had listened to his music and saved him when he was in danger of drowning after being captured by pirates. The dolphin carried Arion to land, and the mast may keep your brother alive until he can reach land."

"Thank you for saying such reassuring words to me," Viola said.

She handed him some money and said, "There is gold for you. My own escape from drowning gives me hope that my brother is still alive, and so do your words — words from someone who knows the sea well."

She added, "Do you know this country of Illyria well?"

"Yes, madam, I do know it well," the captain replied. "I was born and raised not three hours' travel from this very place."

"Who governs here?"

"A noble duke," the captain said. "He is noble both in nature and in name."

"What is his name?"

"Orsino."

"Orsino!" Viola said. "I have heard my father talk about him. He was a bachelor at that time."

"He is still a bachelor," the captain said. "Or at least he was a bachelor until very recently — I have been gone from Illyria for a month. At that time, the gossip was — as you know, the common people gossip about the nobles — that he was seeking the love of fair Olivia."

"Who is she?"

"She is a virtuous maiden, the daughter of a Count who died a year ago, leaving her in the protection of his son, her brother, who shortly afterward died. Because of her love for her brother and her grief over his death, people say that she has decided to shun the company and the sight of men."

"I would like to be employed by that lady and not reveal who I am to the world until I know more certainly what my position and standing in life will be here. I must be cautious because I am a woman in a strange land."

"It will be difficult or impossible to get a position with Countess Olivia," the captain said, "because she has shut herself away and will not listen to any kind of request, not even Duke Orsino's."

"You seem to look and act like a good person, captain. Although some people have an appearance of goodness that hides evil, I believe that your mind suits your fair and outward character. Therefore, I ask you to — and I will pay you well — conceal my identity and aid me as I assume another identity for the time being. I intend to become an employee of Duke Orsino. You shall tell him that I am a eunuch — a castrated male. This will be a win-win-win situation for you, the Duke, and me. I will be a competent employee, and you will get the credit for bringing me to the Duke's attention. I do have talents. I can sing and play musical instruments, and I will provide good value to the Duke. What happens after I enter his employ, only time will tell. But please keep quiet about my identity until I reveal who I really am."

The captain replied, "Go ahead and pretend to be a eunuch, and I will pretend to be a man who is mute and unable to reveal your identity. If I should ever tell your secret, may I go blind."

"Thank you. Now please lead me to Duke Orsino."

Viola thought, *Of course, I may need to alter my plan according to circumstances. If I pretend to be a eunuch, that will explain my lack of beard and my high voice as I sing songs. But if, for some reason, it is not a good idea to pretend to be a eunuch — for example, if Duke Orsino is tired of music — then I can pretend to be a youth who as of yet is incapable of growing a beard. As a young woman, I can manage to assume that identity.*

In Olivia's house, Olivia's personal servant, Maria, and Olivia's alcoholic uncle, Sir Toby Belch, who was staying with Olivia for a while, were talking.

"Why the Devil is my niece so heavily grieving the death of her brother?" Sir Toby Belch said. "Why does she want to mourn him and to stay away from men for the next seven years? I am sure that grief is an enemy to life."

Sir Toby Belch may have been correct in his opinion of excessive grief, but he was a Hell-raiser and a partier and a lover of the drinking of alcohol and the spending of money — especially other people's money. Maria, the personal servant of Olivia, had been sent to Sir Toby to try to convince him to keep regular hours and to party less.

"I swear, Sir Toby, you must start coming home and going to bed earlier. Olivia dislikes your late hours. She takes great exception to them."

"If she wants to except something, then let her make an exception of me," Sir Toby replied.

"You must engage in moderate and orderly conduct. Confine yourself — and your drinking — within reasonable limits."

"Confine? The only thing that I will confine myself in is my clothing! These clothes are good enough to drink in, and so are these boots! If my boots are not good enough to drink in, then they can hang themselves by their own bootstraps."

"Your chugging and drinking will be your downfall. I heard Olivia talk about your drinking yesterday, and I heard her talk about a foolish knight you brought here to woo her and to try to marry her."

"Who? Sir Andrew Aguecheek?"

"Yes, him."

"He is as brave a man as any man in Illyria."

"So what?"

"He's rich. He has an income of three thousand ducats a year."

"True, but he will keep his wealth for only a year. He is a fool and a spendthrift."

"You should not say that," Sir Toby said. "He plays cello, and he speaks three or four languages from memory without having to hold a translating dictionary in his hands, and he has all the good gifts of nature."

"He is a natural, all right," Maria said. "He is a natural fool — if not an idiot. In addition, he is a great quarreler. Fortunately, he also has the gift of being a coward. If not for this gift of retreating from those whom he has angered, all wise and prudent people think that he would quickly receive the gift of a grave."

"The people who say those things are scoundrels and gossip-mongers. Who are these people?"

"These people are those who add that he and you get drunk together each night."

"We get drunk from drinking to the health of my niece, Olivia. I'll drink to her as long as I have a throat and Illyria has alcohol. Anyone who will not drink to Olivia's health until his brain spins like a top is a coward and a knave."

Seeing Sir Andrew coming, Sir Toby said to Maria, "Heads-up. Speaking of the Devil, here comes Sir Andrew Agueface now."

Sir Andrew, who was tall and thin, entered the room and said, "Sir Toby Belch! How are you, Sir Toby?"

"Sweet Sir Andrew! I am well."

To Maria, a very small and very short woman, Sir Andrew said, "Hello, fair shrew."

Unfortunately for Sir Anthony, "shrew" has more than one meaning. He was thinking of a very small mammal, but Maria thought of an evil-tempered woman.

Maria instantly disliked Sir Andrew and instantly realized that all the rumors about him being a fool were true. She had no interest in him, but she would be polite — make that somewhat polite — to him because she was Olivia's personal servant.

She replied, "Hello to you, too, sir."

"Offense," Sir Toby said to Sir Andrew. "Take the offense."

"What are you talking about?" Sir Andrew asked.

"I am talking about this woman, my niece's personal servant."

"Ms. Offense," Sir Andrew said to Maria, "I hope to know you better."

Maria's nickname was Mary, so she said, "My name is Mary, sir."

"That's a good name: Mary Offense —"

Sir Toby said, "You are mistaken, Sir Andrew. Her name is not 'Offense.' I meant for you to take the offense, to mount an attack, and to conquer this woman. Imagine that you are a pirate attacking a ship."

Sir Toby was more than willing to get Sir Andrew to do and say stupid things and expose himself as a fool. Sir Toby knew that Maria's wit was more than adequate to defend herself against whatever offense Sir Andrew would attempt to mount.

"I am not willing to mount this woman," Sir Andrew said. "Heaven forbid that I should mount an attack on a woman!"

Disgusted, Maria said, "Fare you well, gentlemen. I am leaving now."

Sir Toby, "If you let her go so easily and with such a weak offense, you may never have the opportunity to draw your sword again."

Maria smiled faintly. She knew the part of a man's body that Sir Toby was referring to as a "sword."

Sir Andrew said to Maria, "If you leave now, I may never have the opportunity to draw a sword again."

Maria laughed at him.

Sir Andrew did not know why she laughed. He asked, "Do you think that you have fools at hand?"

Maria replied, "Sir, I am not holding your hand."

"But you will," Sir Andrew said, and he grabbed and held her hand.

Maria thought, *And now I have a fool at hand.* She noticed that Sir Andrew's hand was dry like the hand of an old and sexually impotent man.

She said to Sir Andrew, "Whenever a man asks me if he is a fool, I say, 'Thought is free.' But I also think that you should do something to make your hand wet. Bring your hand to the buttery bar and let it drink."

She brought Sir Andrew's hand to just in front of his crotch and thought, *If you smear butter on your hand, it will not be dry. Masturbation ought to make your hand wet and your bar buttery.*

"Why, sweetheart? I don't understand," Sir Andrew said.

"Your hand is dry, sir."

"Yes, it is," Sir Andrew said. "I am not such an ass that I cannot keep my hand dry. Are you making a joke?"

"If I am, it is a dry joke. I have a dry sense of humor."

"Are you full of jokes?"

"I have a joke at the ends of my fingers," Maria said.

She let go of Sir Andrew's hand and said, "Now that I am no longer holding your hand, I no longer have a joke at the ends of my fingers."

She left the room.

Sir Toby said to Sir Andrew, "You need a drink. I have never seen a man so badly defeated by a woman. She really put you down. Have you ever been so put down before?"

"Only when I am put down by too much wine and take up residence under a table," Sir Andrew said. "Sometimes I think that I have no more wit than a Christian or an ordinary man has, but I eat a lot of beef and I think that the fat clogs my brain."

"No doubt about it," Sir Toby sympathized.

"If I believed that, I'd avoid red meat," Sir Andrew replied.

He added, "I am going to leave here tomorrow and go back to my home."

"*Pourquoi*, my dear knight?"

Pourquoi? means "Why?" in French, but Sir Andrew did not know that.

"What does *pourquoi* mean? To leave or not to leave? I wish that I had spent more time learning languages instead of fencing, dancing, and bear-baiting — I love to see savage dogs torment bears! I should have sought an education! I should have been able to curl my tongue around more languages!"

Sir Toby thought, *When I said that Sir Andrew knows three or four languages, I exaggerated. No, I didn't exaggerate — I lied.*

Sir Toby said to Sir Andrew, "If you had learned additional languages, then you would now have an excellent head of hair."

"How would learning more languages improve my hair?"

"A curling-tong would curl it. You can see that your hair is straight."

"My hair is attractive enough as it is, isn't it?"

"Your hair is excellent," Sir Toby said. "It looks like flax being spun straight by a housewife. If the housewife wanted to, she could spin your hair away and then you would be bald. And if the housewife were also a prostitute, she could give you syphilis and then your hair would fall out."

"Ugh," Sir Andrew said. "I am going home tomorrow, Sir Toby. I am here to court your niece, but she will not allow me to see her. Even if I could see her, the odds are four to one against her marrying me; after all, the Duke of Illyria himself wants to marry her."

"Olivia does not want to marry Orsino," Sir Toby said, "She will not marry anyone above her in wealth, age, or intelligence. I have heard her swear it. Don't worry. You still have a chance to marry her. Where there's life, there's hope."

"I will stay a month longer," Sir Andrew decided. "I can change my mind very quickly. I delight in masquerades with music and dancing and I delight in partying — sometimes all at the same time."

"Are you good at dancing?"

"I am as good as any man in Illyria, whoever he is, as long as his social standing is not above mine. Still, it is true that I am not as good as an old man who is experienced at dancing."

"Can you dance a lively five-stepped dance?"

"I can cut a caper."

"And I can cut the mutton to go with your caper," Sir Andrew said, thinking of the little peppery berries — capers — that are often served with mutton.

"I can also dance backwards."

"Why are you hiding these talents of yours?" Sir Toby asked. "It is like you have put curtains in front of them to keep the dust off the way we put curtains in front of paintings to protect them. Why don't you dance on your way to church, and after church is over dance a different dance on your way back home? If I were you, I would dance instead of walk. I would dance even while going to a bathroom. I would dance a sink-a-pace — oops, I mean the French dance called *cinquepace* — up to a sink and then I would pee in it. What do you mean by hiding your talent for dancing? Is this the kind of world you ought to hide virtues in? When I saw your legs, I immediately knew that you were born to dance."

"Yes, my legs are strong," Sir Andrew said, "and they look good in stockings. Shall we do some reveling?"

"What else?" Sir Toby said. "Weren't both of us born under the astrological sign of Taurus?"

"Doesn't Taurus rule the sides and heart?"

"No, sir, it rules the legs and thighs," Sir Toby said.

Actually, Taurus is supposed to rule the neck and throat. Sir Andrew got it wrong through ignorance. Sir Toby got it wrong so he could laugh at Sir Andrew.

Sir Toby said, "Let me see you dance a caper."

Sir Andrew began dancing.

"That's it! Move your knees higher! Higher!"

Viola had put her plan in action. She had dressed in male clothing and was now working for Duke Orsino. However, she had abandoned the idea of being a eunuch and instead simply called herself a youth — a youth by the name of Cesario. Now she was in Duke Orsino's palace talking with one of his assistants: Valentine.

Valentine said, "If the Duke continues to show favor to you, Cesario, you are likely to advance far and quickly. He has known you only three days, and already he treats you as a favorite and not as a stranger."

Viola, who was dressed in male clothing, said, "You say 'if.' You must either fear that Orsino will change his mind about me or that I will neglect my duties and so he may no longer show favor to me. Does he quickly change his opinion about people?"

"No, he does not," Valentine said. "You have my word on that."

"Thank you. I see him coming now."

Duke Orsino, his attendant Curio, and others entered the room.

"Has anyone seen Cesario?" Orsino asked.

"Here I am, and at your service," Viola said.

Orsino said to Valentine, Curio, and the others, "Stand at a distance for a while. I want to speak to Cesario privately."

He then said to Viola, "You know no less than everything about me. I have even told you my secrets. You know whom I love: Olivia. Therefore, go to her. Do not allow yourself to be denied to see her. Stand at her door, and tell the servants at her doors that your feet are fixed there and you will not leave until you have seen and talked to Olivia."

"My noble lord," Viola said, "if Olivia is much in sorrow and in grieving for her dead brother, as I have heard, it is likely that she will not allow me to see her."

"Insist on it. Act like a jerk if you have to, but be sure to see her before you return to my palace."

"Suppose I am able to speak to her, sir. What do you want me to tell her?"

"Tell her about my passionate love for her," Orsino said. "Overwhelm her with stories about me that will capture her heart. You are the proper messenger for this. She will pay more attention to you, a youth, than she would to an older messenger."

"I doubt that, sir," Viola said.

"Youth, believe it," Orsino replied. "Anyone who calls you a man is mistaken. You are not yet old enough to be a man. Your lips are as smooth and as ruby-red as the lips of the virgin goddess Diana. Your boyish voice is like the voice of a maiden, high and unbroken. Everything about you is feminine. I know that you are the right messenger and have the right personality for this affair."

Orsino said to his attendants, "Four or five of you go with Cesario on his errand — no, all of you go with him. I like it best when I am alone."

He said to Viola, "If you perform this errand well, you will prosper. You shall live as well as I do with all of my resources."

Viola replied, "I'll do my best to woo the lady and make her yours."

But she thought, *This is a disagreeable errand. I will be wooing a woman for Orsino to make his wife, but I have fallen in love with him and I want the woman he marries to be me!*

Maria, who had recently used her wits to reveal the foolishness of Sir Andrew Aguecheek, was in Olivia's house talking to a person of wit and intelligence. This person was Feste, a jester who made his living by making other people laugh. Some people called him a clown, and some people called him a fool. He was funny like so many clowns are, and he was wise like so many "fools" are. He served Olivia and occasionally picked up tips at other people's houses, and he had been away from Olivia's house for a long time.

Maria said to Feste, "Either tell me where you have been for so long, or I will not utter a word in your defense. You have been away for so long that Olivia is likely to have you hanged."

Both Maria and Feste knew that this was an exaggeration. But if Olivia really would be angry enough to want to have Feste hanged, her face would be an angry red.

Feste replied, "Let her hang me: he that is well hanged in this world need fear no colors."

Maria smiled. She knew that "well hanged" meant "well hung."

She said, "Explain what you mean by 'fear no colors.'"

"A hung man is a dead man, and he will see no colors."

"That is a good Lenten answer, Feste. Lent is a time of fasting, and your answer lacks substance. You have made a lame joke with no meat on it."

She added, "I can tell you where the saying 'I fear no colors' comes from."

"From where, Mistress Mary?" Feste asked.

"From the wars," Maria said. "Soldiers wear colored uniforms, and they march under a colored flag. Someone who fears no colors is not afraid of the enemy. When you face Olivia, who will be angry because of your long absence, you will be facing the enemy, and you better hope that you fear no colors."

"Well, may God give more wisdom to those who already have it. As for those who are fools, let them use whatever talents they have."

"As I said, you will be hanged because you have been absent for so long," Maria said, "or you will be fired and lack employment. Won't that be the same as a hanging to you?"

Feste said, "Many a good hanging prevents a bad marriage."

Maria smiled. She knew the proverb "Better be half hanged than ill married." She also thought that a man's being well hung might be advantageous in keeping a wife happy.

Feste added, "As for being fired, it is summer and that will make unemployment bearable."

"You are resolute not to tell me where you have been?"

"Not necessarily," Feste said, "but I am braced to make two points."

"Those two points are the places where your braces — your suspenders — are attached to buttons so they can keep your pants up. If only one point suffers a mishap and the button comes off, the other point will keep your pants up. But if you lose both buttons, you will also lose your pants."

"Well jested," Feste said. "Go about your business now, but let me say that if Sir Toby would stop drinking, he would realize that you are as witty as any daughter of Eve in Illyria. He might even realize that just as Eve became Adam's wife, you could be a clever wife for him."

Maria replied, "Hold your tongue. I don't want to hear any more of that. Look. Here comes Olivia. You had better come up with a good way to explain to her why you have been absent for so long."

Maria left the room as Olivia and Malvolio, Olivia's dignified and dutiful steward, entered it. Malvolio was not the type of person to take a long authorized leave of absence the way that Feste had. A few other male servants also entered the room.

Feste thought to himself, *I need to be witty so that Olivia will cease her anger at me for being away for so long. If I can make her laugh, I won't get fired.*

He said to himself, being sure that he spoke loud enough for Olivia to overhear him, "Wit, if it be thy will, make me funny. Just as ancient epic poets invoked the Muses and asked them for help in telling their tales, I am invoking Wit and asking it for inspiration. Many wits who think that they are witty very often prove to be fools. I am sure that I lack wit, and since I am aware of what I lack, I may pass for a wise man, just as Socrates did. What does the great philosopher Kungfooey say? 'Better a witty fool, than a foolish wit!'"

He looked at Olivia and said, "God bless thee, lady!"

She was not happy with him. She said, "Take the fool away."

Feste said, "Didn't you hear her, fellows? Take away the lady."

"Go away," Olivia said. "I want nothing more to do with you. For one thing, you have grown unreliable. A major part of success is simply showing up, and you have not been doing that recently. Apparently, your wit has dried up. You, Feste, are a dry fool."

"You have mentioned two faults, lady, that drink and good advice can mend," Feste replied. "Give a dry fool a drink, and he will no longer be dry. Bid a man with chronic absence to mend himself, and if he does mend himself, he is no longer chronically absent, but if he does not mend himself, let a tailor mend him. Anything that's mended is patched. If a virtuous man is mended, he is patched with sin. If a sinful man is mended, he is patched with virtue. If this simple argument is valid, well and good. If it is not valid, what would be the remedy? Olivia, the only true cuckold is calamity. People are wedded to fortune, and when fortune turns bad and is unfaithful to them, they become the equivalents of cuckolds. So, Olivia, turn away from calamity — turn away from excessive mourning for your late brother. The living must return to living. Know that beauty is a flower. It will not last. Enjoy the flower of your beauty, Olivia, and marry before your flower fades. *Carpe diem*, for all of us must one day die. Olivia has been behaving like a fool; therefore, I say again, take her away."

Olivia replied, "Sir, I bade them to take away *you*."

"Then you have made an error of the very worst kind," Feste said. "You have called me a fool, and it is true that I am wearing motley, which is the costume of a fool, but I do not wear motley in my brain. Good lady, give me permission to prove to you that you are a fool."

"Can you do it?"

"With ease, good lady," Feste replied.

"Prove it."

"I will do so with a catechism. I will ask you questions, and you will answer them honestly."

"Well, sir, for lack of a better entertainment, I will do so."

"Good lady, why do you mourn?"

"Good fool, I mourn because of my brother's death."

"I think his soul is in Hell, good lady."

"I know his soul is in Heaven, fool."

"Then you must be a fool, good lady, to mourn because your brother's soul is in Heaven."

Feste turned to the male servants and said, "Take away the fool, gentlemen."

Pleased with Feste, Olivia said, "What do you think of this fool, Malvolio? Hasn't he mended himself?"

"Yes, he does mend, and he shall continue to mend until the pangs of death shake him," Malvolio, who did not like Feste's long absence and dereliction of duty, said. "Infirmity, that decays the wise, does ever make the better fool. Senility makes fools of even the wisest."

"God send you, sir, a speedy infirmity, for the betterment of your folly!" Feste, who was fighting — very well — for his job and did not want Olivia to hear Malvolio's criticisms of him, replied. "Sir Toby is willing to swear that I am not a sly and cunning and dangerous fox, but he will not bet even two pennies that you are not a fool."

"What do you say to that, Malvolio?" Olivia asked.

"I marvel that your ladyship takes delight in such an uninspired rascal as Feste," Malvolio replied. "I saw him defeated in a battle of wits the other day by an ordinary fool who has no more brains than a stone. Look at him now. He has shrugged his shoulders and turned away. Unless you laugh and thereby encourage him to make jokes, he is gagged and unable to say anything. I swear that I regard so-called wise men, who crow with laughter at these professional fools, as being no better than the fools' sidekicks."

"Oh, you are sick with self-love and pride, Malvolio, and you taste with a sick appetite," Olivia said. "You are unable to appreciate what a jester does. You ought to be generous and liberal-minded, guiltless, and good-natured. You ought to regard as blunted arrows all those things that you now regard as cannonballs. A professional fool such as Feste commits no slander, even when he says nothing but abuse and criticism. A good jester will speak truth to power — and make that truth funny, too. A good fool can give good advice while making bad — and sometimes good — puns. That is a part of his job. And a man such as yourself who is known for his sound judgment is not a ranting lunatic even when he criticizes and complains. That is a part of your job. You have sound judgment, and that sound judgment can result in sound criticism."

Feste said to Olivia, "May Mercury, the god of deception, give you the gift of lying well because you have spoken so kindly of fools. If you are going to talk well about fools, you need to be able to lie well."

Maria entered the room and said to Olivia, "Madam, there is at the gate a young gentleman who much desires to speak with you."

"Count Orsino sent him, didn't he?"

"I don't know, madam. He is a handsome young man, and he has some other men with him."

"Who is talking to him now and keeping him from entering this house?"

"Sir Toby, madam, your uncle."

"Keep Sir Toby away from the young man, please. Sir Toby — darn him! — speaks as if he were a madman."

Maria left to talk to Sir Toby.

Olivia said, "Take care of this, Malvolio. If Orsino sent this young man, get rid of him. Tell him that I am sick or not at home. Say whatever you have to — just get rid of him."

Malvolio left the room to talk to the young man.

Olivia said to Feste, "You can see that some people think that your fooling has grown stale, and they dislike it."

Feste replied, "You have spoken up in favor of fools, madam, just as if your oldest son, if you had one, wanted to be a fool and you were defending him. May Jove — the god Jupiter — stuff the head of your oldest son — when you have one — with brains. He may need the extra help because one of your relatives has a very weak brain — look! Here he comes!"

Sir Toby Belch entered the room.

Olivia said to Feste, "I swear that he is already half-drunk."

She asked Sir Toby, "Who was at the gate?"

"A gentleman."

"I know that. Which gentleman?"

"He is a gentleman —"

Sir Toby belched and then said, "Darn these pickled herrings!"

He saw Feste and said, "How are you, fool?"

"I am well, good Sir Toby."

Olivia said, "Sir Toby, you are practically in a drunken stupor. It's still early in the day. Why are you so early in a state of lethargy?"

Sir Toby misheard her, or pretended to: "Lechery! I defy lechery!"

Then he added, "There is someone at the gate."

"Who is he?" Olivia asked.

"He can be the Devil, if he wants," Sir Toby replied. "I don't care. Give me faith, and that will protect me from the Devil. Well, it doesn't matter."

Sir Toby left the room.

Olivia asked Feste, "What is a drunken man like, fool?"

"A drunken man is like a fool, a madman, and a drowned man. One drink too many makes him a fool. Two drinks too many make him a madman. Three drinks too many drown him."

"Go and find a coroner, and let him hold an inquest on Sir Toby because Sir Toby has had three drinks too many — he has drowned. Go, and look after Sir Toby."

"Sir Toby is only a madman right now," Feste said. "The fool shall look after the madman."

Feste left to keep an eye on Sir Toby. Feste knew that his job was now secure.

Malvolio entered the room and said to Olivia, "The young fellow outside swears that he will not leave until he speaks to you. I told him that you were sick. He said that he knew that and that was why he needed to speak to you. I told him that you were asleep. He said that he knew that and that was why he needed to speak to you. What can I say to him, lady? Whatever I say to him, he has an answer, and he will not leave."

"Tell him that he cannot speak to me."

"I have told him that, and he says that he will stand at your door as if he were one of the columns holding up the porch roof or as if he were one of the legs of a bench outdoors. He says that he will not leave until after he has spoken to you."

"What kind of man is he?"

"Just an ordinary man."

"What manner of man?"

"He is an ill-mannered man. He says that he will speak to you whether you want him to or not."

"What is his appearance, and how old is he?"

"He is not yet a man and no longer a boy. He is like a peapod or an apple just before it ripens. He stands between being a man and being a boy.

He is good-looking, and he speaks very sharply. He speaks as if he were an ill-tempered young child who has just been forced to stop drinking his mother's milk."

"Let him come in and talk to me. Call in Maria to be with me and be a chaperone."

Malvolio called, "Maria, Olivia wants you to come here."

Maria walked into the room.

Olivia said, "Give me my veil. Throw it over my face. Once again, I will listen to one of Orsino's ambassadors."

Maria also put on a veil. This made it difficult for Viola to tell who was the lady of the house and who was the servant.

Viola came into the room, accompanied by a few attendants.

She asked, "Who is the lady of the house?"

Olivia replied, "Speak to me; I shall answer for her. What do you want?"

Viola began to recite a speech that she had written: "Most radiant, exquisite, and unmatchable beauty."

She stopped and then said to Maria, "Please, tell me if this woman is the lady of the house because I have never seen the lady of the house. I would hate to recite my speech to the wrong person because it is a very good speech and I have taken great pains to memorize it."

Viola said to both Olivia and Maria, "Good beauties, do not mock me. I am very sensitive, and I feel even the smallest unkindness."

"From where have you come, sir?" Olivia asked.

"I am here to recite my speech," Viola said. "The answer to your question is not part of my speech."

She added, "Gentle lady, please tell me whether you are the lady of the house, so that if you are I can proceed with my speech."

"Are you an actor?" Olivia asked.

"No, my wise little sweetheart, I am not a professional actor," Viola said.

She thought, *And yet, in the teeth of ill fate, I swear that I am not the person whose part I play.*

Then she asked again, "Are you the lady of the house?"

"If I do not usurp myself, I am," Olivia replied.

"If you are the lady of the house, then you usurp herself," Viola said. "You wrongfully possess your own person. What is yours to give is not yours to keep.

You ought to give yourself to a husband. But I ought to be reciting my speech, and I am not doing that. I will continue with my praise of you in my speech, and then I will tell you the heart — the important part — of the message."

"Just tell me the important part," Olivia said. "You may skip the praise."

"But, lady," Viola objected. "I worked hard to memorize the praise, and it is poetic."

"The more poetic it is, the more likely it is to be fake," Olivia said. "Please keep the praise to yourself. I heard that you were rude when you were at my gate. I allowed you to see me because I wanted to marvel at such a rude person — not because I wanted to hear what you have to say. If you are insane, go away; if you have reason, be brief. I am not so lunatic that I want to be a part of an insane conversation."

Maria said to Viola, "Will you hoist sail, sir? Here lies your way."

She pointed to the door.

"No, good swabber of decks. I intend to cast anchor here for a while longer," Viola said to Maria.

Viola said to Olivia about Maria, who was a very short woman, "Please pacify your threatening giant, sweet lady."

She added, "Are you willing to hear my message?"

Olivia said, "You must have some hideous message to deliver, since you are ill mannered. Tell me what you have to say."

"It alone concerns your ear," Viola said. "I bring no declaration of war, no demand for tribute: I hold the olive branch in my hand; my words are as full of peace as they are full of content."

"Yet you have behaved rudely. Who are you? What do you want?"

"The rudeness that has been apparent in me I have learned from the way I have been treated here. Who I am, and what I want, are as secret as virginity. My message is for your ears only. To you, my message is divine. To others, my message is profane."

Olivia said to the other people in the room, "Let this young man and me be alone. I will hear his divine message to me."

Maria and the others left the room.

Olivia said, "You said that you have something divine to tell me. What is your text? What is the gospel passage that you will preach about?"

Viola began, "Most sweet lady —"

Olivia interrupted, "That is a comfortable doctrine — it brings comfort to me. Much may be said in favor of your text. Next question: Where lies your text?"

"In the chest of Orsino."

"In his chest!" Olivia said. "That's an interesting place for a text. In what chapter of his chest?"

"To continue your use of biblical exegesis, it lies in the foremost place in his heart."

"I have read that text," Olivia said. "It is heresy. Have you anything more to say?"

"Good madam, let me see your face."

"Has Orsino told you to negotiate with my face? You are now departing from your text — that is, straying from your theme — but I will draw the curtain and show you the picture you want to see."

She took off her veil, and then she said, "Look at my face now. This is the way I look at the present time. Think of my face as a portrait. Don't you think that it is well done?"

Viola replied, "It is excellently done, if God did all that I see and you have had no help from cosmetics."

"Everything you see is natural. Cosmetics wash off, but my face will endure wind and weather."

"Then your beauty has a truly beautiful blending of colors: the red of your lips and cheeks and the white of your face. Nature has painted your face with paint that is not artificial. Lady, you are the cruelest woman alive if you will take your beauty to the grave and leave the world no copy."

"Sir, I will not be so hard-hearted. I will give the world more than one copy. I will give several lists of my beauty — it shall be inventoried, and every item and every part will be added as a codicil to my will. Item: two lips, red. Item: two grey eyes, with lids. Item: one neck. Item: one chin. And so forth."

"I meant that you should leave behind you a copy in the form of a child."

"Were you sent here just to praise my beauty?"

"I can see that you are too proud, but even if you were as proud as the Devil, you are beautiful. Orsino, my master, loves you. Such love would receive no more than its due even if you were crowned with the title of the unequalled Queen of Beauty!"

"How does he love me?"

"He loves you with adorations, abundant tears, with groans that thunder love, and with sighs of fiery heat."

"Orsino knows what I think about him. I cannot love him. Yet I suppose him to be virtuous, and I know that he is noble. He is wealthy, and he is a fresh and stainless youth. He is well spoken of and has a good reputation. He is generous, and he is well educated and courageous. Physically, he is a graceful and attractive person. Nevertheless, I do not love him. He should know that; he has certainly heard it for a long time."

"If I loved you the way that Orsino — a martyr to love — loves you, and if I suffered the way that he suffers because of his love for you, I would not be able to understand why you refuse to return his love. I would find no sense in such a refusal."

"And what would you do if you were Orsino?" Olivia asked.

"Willows are the emblems of unrequited love. I would make for myself a willow cabin at your gate, and I would call upon my soul — that is, you — within your house. I would write songs about a faithful love that is not returned, and I would sing them loudly even in the middle of night. I would shout your name to the echoing hills and make the air call your name: 'Olivia!' The nymph Echo would continually be at my service and help me make the air sound your name. No matter where you would go, you would pity me."

Olivia thought, *I would like that — a lot. I want to know this young man better — much better.*

She said, "Doing such things might get you somewhere. Who are your parents?"

"My parents' social rank was above that of my present social rank, yet I am doing well. I am a gentleman."

"Return to Orsino and tell him that I cannot love him. Tell him to send no more messengers to me, unless, perhaps, you come to me again to tell me how Orsino takes my message. Fare you well. I thank you for your pains: Spend this for me."

She held out money for Viola to take, but Viola declined to take it.

She said, "I am no messenger who needs a tip, lady; keep your money. It is Orsino, not myself, who lacks recompense. He gets no return for the love he has spent. May you fall in love with someone who has a heart of flint, and may that someone regard with contempt your love, the way you regard with contempt Orsino's love. Farewell, fair cruelty."

Viola left the room to return to Orsino.

Olivia said to herself, "I asked him about his parents, and he said that their social rank was above that of his present social rank and that he is a gentleman. I can well believe that he is a gentleman. His manner of speaking, face, limbs, actions, and spirit provide five proofs that he is a gentleman. But, Olivia, slow down! You could go fast if this young man were Orsino and Orsino were the servant. What is happening to me? Can I be falling in love so quickly? This young man has perfections that invisibly and stealthily are creeping into my mind. Well, I am in love. So be it."

She took a ring off her finger and called, "Malvolio!"

Malvolio entered the room and said, "Here I am, madam, at your service."

"Run after that stubborn messenger, Orsino's servant. He left this ring behind him, with no regard to whether or not I wanted it. Tell him that I don't want it. Tell him not to flatter Orsino that I may love him — tell him not to give Orsino any hope that I may love him. I do not love Orsino. If that young messenger will come tomorrow, he can tell me how Orsino takes my rejection of his love for me. Hurry, Malvolio, and catch up to the young messenger."

"Madam, I will," Malvolio said, and he left the room.

"I am not sure what I am doing," Olivia said to herself. "I am afraid that I am falling in love with this young man's good looks and that I am not using my mind. Fate, you are in control — we do not control ourselves. Whatever will be, will be."

CHAPTER 2

— 3.1 —

Viola's twin brother, Sebastian, had survived the shipwreck. Now he was on the coast, talking with the person who had saved his life and who had given him food and shelter: Antonio.

Antonio asked, "Won't you stay longer here? And if you must go, will you allow me to go with you?"

Sebastian replied, "I am sorry, but I must leave, and I must not allow you to go with me. My astrological stars shine darkly over me, and my fate is malignant. If you go with me, my bad luck may affect you; therefore, I must ask you to allow me to travel alone. I would repay your kindness badly if I were to share my bad fortune with you."

"At least let me know where you are bound."

"My plan is to simply wander here and there. I do not know where I will end up. I see, however, that you have good manners, and they prevent you from asking questions about myself because you are afraid that you will ask about something that I do not want to talk about. Etiquette demands that I tell you about myself. You ought to know that my real name is Sebastian. Out of caution, I have been using the alias Roderigo. My father was Sebastian of Messaline, a man I know you have heard of. When he died, he left behind him my sister and me. We were twins; we were both born in the same hour — I wish to God that we had both died in the same hour! But you, sir, prevented that. You rescued me from the sea that drowned my sister."

"I am sorry that she drowned."

"Although she was said to resemble me, many people thought that she was beautiful. That may have been generous praise, but I can say without reservation to anybody and everybody that her mind was so good and intelligent that even an envious person would have to admit that that is true. My sister drowned in the salt water of the sea, and my salty tears drown her memory each time I think of her."

"Pardon me, sir, for not giving you better hospitality."

"Forgive me, Antonio, for the trouble I have given to you."

Antonio deeply loved Sebastian as a friend.

Antonio said, "Unless you want me to die out of grief because you are leaving me, allow me to be your servant and go with you."

"Don't ask that. It would kill me — thereby undoing your heroic act of saving my life — if you were to suffer from my bad fortune by going with me. I am filled with tenderness toward you, and I am enough like my mother that I too easily cry and show my feelings. But now I will set out on the first part of my wanderings. I am going to the court of Orsino, the Duke of Illyria. Goodbye."

Sebastian departed, and Antonio said to himself, "May the gods protect you! I have many enemies in the court of Duke Orsino; otherwise, I would go there and see you. But, come what may, I do adore you so, that danger shall seem to be like entertainment, and I will go. So, off I will go to Court Orsino's town, where I intend to see you."

Viola walked on a street, and Malvolio, walking more quickly than she, caught up with her.

Malvolio said to Viola, "Are you the young man who was just now talking with the Countess Olivia?"

"Yes, I was, sir. I have been walking and have just now arrived here."

"Olivia returns this ring to you, sir. You would have saved me the trouble of walking after you, if you had taken it away yourself. She adds, moreover, that you should tell Orsino very clearly that she wants nothing to do with him. One more thing: Olivia does not want you to deliver any more declarations of love from Orsino, although she will allow you to report to her how Orsino takes her rejection of his love for her. Now, take back this ring."

Viola knew that she had left no ring for Olivia; therefore, this must be Olivia's ring; however, Viola did not want to reveal that information to Malvolio.

Viola said, "Olivia took the ring. I want nothing to do with it."

Malvolio replied, "Come, sir, you peevishly threw it to her; and she wants to return it to you."

He dropped the ring on the ground and said, "There the ring lies. If it is worth stooping for, pick it up. If you don't want to pick it up, let it become the property of whoever finds it."

Malvolio departed.

Viola picked up the ring and said, "I left no ring with Olivia. What does she mean by this? God forbid that she has fallen in love with me. My disguise has fooled her! She certainly stared at me when we were alone together. Indeed, she stared so much that she became distracted and spoke in starts and did not finish her sentences. Sometimes, she lost the power of speech. She is in love with me, and she is crafty enough to send this churlish messenger to me to make an invitation to visit her again. She says that she does not want the ring of Orsino — why, he did not give her a ring! I am the 'man' she loves! If this is true, and it is, then I feel pity for Olivia. She would be better off if she loved a dream. Disguise, I see, is wicked, and the Devil uses it to make mischief. How easy is it for handsome and deceitful men to imprint themselves on the hearts of women just like a seal imprints itself on wax! It's a pity, but the frailty of us women is the cause of our susceptibility to fall in love — we ourselves are not the cause! We are made this way, and neither Olivia nor I can help falling in love. How will this turn out? Orsino has fallen in love with Olivia, I — a woman dressed in men's clothing — have fallen in love with Orsino, and poor Olivia, who thinks that I am a man, seems to have fallen in love with me. What will become of this? I am a monster: part man and part woman. Since I am disguised as a man, I cannot gain the love of Orsino. Since I really am a woman, Olivia cannot gain my love. She shall sigh hopelessly out of unrequited love. Time, you must untangle this, not I; it is too hard a knot for me to untie!"

— 2.3 —

In Olivia's house, Sir Toby Belch and Sir Andrew Aguecheek were partying. As usual, they had drunk too much.

Sir Toby said, "Come here, Sir Andrew. We are not in bed although it is after midnight, and therefore we are up early. And, of course, *deliculo surgere saluberrimum est* — to rise early is very healthy. I am sure that you know that."

"No, I do not know that. Latin is another language I do not know. But I do know this: To be up late is to be up late."

"That is a false conclusion. I hate it the way I hate an empty tankard. To be up after midnight is to be up early — it is in the early hours of the morning. Therefore, to go to bed after midnight is to go to bed early. So say the ancient scholars. Do not the ancient scholars also say that our life consists of the four elements: fire, air, water, and earth?"

"Yes, they say that, but I think that life consists of eating and drinking."

"I prefer your scholarship to that of the ancient scholars," Sir Toby said.

He called, "Maria! Bring us a jug of wine!"

Feste entered the room and said, "How are you, my friends! Have you ever seen the picture of 'We Three'?"

The picture Feste referred to showed two fools or asses — the third fool or ass was the person looking at the picture.

Sir Toby replied, "Welcome, ass. Now let's have a song."

Feste's talents included playing musical instruments and singing and dancing.

Sir Andrew said, "Truly, the fool has an excellent singing voice. I would give a large amount of money to be able to play and sing and dance as well as this fool can."

He said to Feste, "Truly, last night you were very funny. You spoke wonderful nonsense about Pigrogromitus and the Vapians passing the equator of Queubus. That tale was very good entertainment. I sent you sixpence to spend on your girlfriend — did you get it?"

Sir Andrew had praised Feste's nonsense, so Feste replied with nonsense to thank him: "I did impeticos thy gratillity, for Malvolio's nose is no whipstock. My lady has a white hand, and the Myrmidons are no bottle-ale houses."

"Excellent!" Sir Andrew said. "Why, this is the best fooling, and the best entertainment, when all is said and done. Now, let's hear a song!"

"Good idea," Sir Toby said, handing Feste some money. "There is sixpence for you. Let's have a song."

"Here is sixpence from me, too," Sir Andrew said. "If one knight gives a sixpence, the second knight ought to, too."

Feste asked, "Do you prefer a love song or a song of the good and simple life in the countryside?"

"A love song, a love song," Sir Toby said.

"I agree," Sir Andrew said. "I don't care for a good and simple life."

Feste sang, "*Oh, mistress mine, where are you roaming?*
"*Oh, stay and hear; your true love's coming,*
"*Who can sing both high and low.*
"*Trip no further, pretty sweeting;*
"*Journeys end in lovers meeting,*
"*Every wise man's son does know.*"

Feste thought, *Wise men — and wise women — seek love.*

Sir Andrew said, "Excellent."

Sir Toby added, "Good, good."

Feste sang, "*What is love? 'tis not hereafter;*
"*Present mirth has present laughter.*
"*What's to come is still unsure:*
"*In delay there lies no plenty;*
"*Then come kiss me, sweet and twenty,*
"*Youth's a stuff that will not endure.*"

Feste thought, *Seize the day. Carpe diem. Youth is fleeting, so enjoy it. Neither Orsino nor Olivia is now doing that.*

Sir Andrew was full of praise for Feste's singing: "He has a mellifluous voice — this I swear as a true knight."

Sir Toby said, "He sang a catchy tune — it is contagious."

Sir Andrew said, "It is sweet and contagious."

Sir Toby said, "If we could hear the tune with our nose, we would enjoy catching a cold."

He added, "What shall we do now? Shall we drink until the sky spins in circles? Shall we sing and keep the night owl up late — and early? Love songs are supposed to draw souls out of the body because of the songs' wickedness, so I'm not sure why weavers sing psalms — love songs to God — as they work. Shall we sing a three-singer song that will draw our souls out of our bodies? Shall we do that?"

"Please, let's do it," Sir Andrew said. "I am as expert at singing catchy songs as a dog is at whatever a dog does."

Feste said, "Like you, a dog is an expert when it comes to a catch."

"That is true," Sir Andrew said, "Let our catchy three-singer song be 'Hold Your Peace, Knave, and I Beg that You Hold Your Peace.'"

"Hold Your Peace" was a riotous party song.

"In this song, each of the singers takes turns singing," Feste said, "and each of the singers calls the other singers 'knave.' Is it all right if I call you a knave, knight?"

"It won't be the first time that I have been called a knave," Sir Andrew said. "You start the song, fool. It goes, 'Hold your peace.'"

"If I hold my peace, I will have to remain silent," Feste said. "I will never be able to get started singing."

"That funny!" Sir Andrew said. "But, now, begin."

The three partiers sang, and in their song two drunks and one fool called each other names and told each other to shut up.

Maria walked into the room and said to Sir Toby, "What a caterwauling you are making! Olivia must be awakening her steward, Malvolio, and ordering him to kick you out of her house. If she isn't, never again believe anything I say."

Sir Toby replied drunkenly, "Olivia is from China, we are politicians, and Malvolio has his nose to the grindstone. Olivia is a Confucian and concerned about order, we are cunning schemers who want preferential treatment, and Malvolio's nose bleeds."

He sang, "*Three merry men be we.*"

He then asked Maria, "Aren't I related to Olivia? Aren't she and I niece and uncle? Fiddle-faddle. I don't need to worry about Olivia."

He sang, "*There dwelt a man in Babylon, lady, lady!*"

"Heaven help me," Feste said to Sir Andrew. "Sir Toby makes an excellent clown."

"Yes, he does it well enough when he is in the mood," Sir Andrew said. "So do I. He acts the clown with a good deal of style. I do it more naturally."

Yes, Feste thought. *You act the clown as if you were a born idiot.*

Sir Toby sang, "*Oh, the twelfth day of December.*"

Maria said, "For the love of God, be quiet!"

Malvolio entered the room and said, "My masters, are you mad? If not, what are you? Have you no wit, manners, or decency that would stop you from gabbling like foul-mouthed, drunken tinkers at this time of night? Do you think Olivia's house is an alehouse where you can squeak out your cobblers' songs at the top of your voices? Is there no respect of place, persons, or time — it is past midnight — in you?"

Sir Toby replied, "We do respect time — we did keep time, sir, in our songs. We have good rhythm. Go hang yourself!"

Malvolio replied, "Sir Toby, I must be blunt with you. My lady told me to tell you, that, though she has given you a place to stay because you are her uncle, she dislikes your disorders. If you can separate yourself from your misdemeanors, you are welcome to stay in her house; if not, and if it would please you to take leave of her, she is very willing to tell you goodbye."

Sir Toby sang, "*Farewell, dear heart, since I must needs be gone.*"

"No, good Sir Toby," Maria said. "Don't sing."

Feste sang the next line of the song: "*His eyes do show his days are almost done.*"

"Must you continue to sing?" Malvolio asked.

Sir Toby sang, "*But I will never die.*"

Feste made up an additional lyric: "*Sir Toby, there you lie.*"

Malvolio said sarcastically, "Your behavior does you credit."

Sir Toby sang, "*Shall I tell him to go?*"

Feste sang, "*What happens if you do?*"

"*Shall I tell him to go and not mince my words?*" Sir Toby sang.

"*Oh, no, no, no, no, you dare not,*" Feste sang.

Sir Toby said to Malvolio, "Are we singing out of time? Not with our rhythm! You lied! You are nothing more than an employee — a steward!"

He added, "Do you think, because you are virtuous, there shall be no more cakes and ale?"

For Sir Toby, it was always time for cakes and ale and parties. For Olivia and for Malvolio, it was not time for cakes and ale and parties when Olivia was trying to sleep.

Feste said, "Very definitely, sometime is the right time for cakes and ale. Hot ale spiced with ginger warms the mouth. Saint Anne, the mother of the Virgin Mary, knew the importance of wine. Jesus' first miracle was turning water into wine so that a wedding could be properly celebrated."

Sir Toby said to Feste, "You are right."

Feste favored Sir Toby over Malvolio — Sir Toby gave him tips.

Feste had been drinking — a lot — and as Sir Toby continued to argue with Malvolio, Feste began to nod and then to sleep.

Sir Toby said to Malvolio, "Go and rub your steward's chain with crumbs to polish it. You are only a servant."

He said to Maria, "Bring us a jug of wine, Maria."

Maria got a jug of wine for Sir Toby, whom she liked.

Malvolio said to Maria, "If you prized Olivia's wishes and did not have contempt for them, Mistress Mary, you would not bring more wine out to encourage this uncivil behavior. I shall tell Olivia what you have done."

Malvolio departed.

After Malvolio had gone, Maria said in the direction of the door he had exited through, "You have donkey ears. Go and shake them."

Sir Andrew said, "I think that it would be an excellent idea to challenge a man to a duel and then not show up and so make a fool of him. I would like to make a fool of Malvolio."

"Do it," Sir Toby said, thinking that Sir Andrew fighting would be a funny sight. "You are a knight, after all. I will write your challenge to Malvolio for you, or if you prefer, I will deliver your challenge orally."

Maria said, "Sweet Sir Toby, be calm, quiet, and patient for tonight. Since Duke Orsino's young man talked with your niece Olivia, she has been much disturbed and distracted. As for Monsieur Malvolio, leave him to me. If I do not trick him, do not think that I am intelligent enough to lie straight in my bed. I intend to make the name 'Malvolio' a synonym for 'laughingstock.' I know that I can do it."

"Tell us something about Malvolio," Sir Toby said. "What characteristics of his can you use to trick him?"

"Sir, sometimes he is a kind of Puritan. He affects a puritanical demeanor. He is morally narrow-minded and thinks that everyone else ought to be, too."

Sir Andrew said, "If I thought that, I would beat him like a dog."

"What, for being a Puritan?" Sir Toby said. "What is your ingenious reason for wanting to beat him?"

"I have no ingenious reason, but I have reason good enough."

Maria said, "Malvolio is not a Puritan; he is a kind of Puritan. Sometimes, he acts like a Puritan. Sometimes, he does not. He is a time-server — he changes his views to suit the prevailing circumstances or fashion. He is nothing consistently except for being an affected ass who learns rules by heart and quotes them at great length. He has the highest opinion of himself, and he thinks that he is so crammed with excellent qualities that he believes with all his heart that all those who see him like him."

An impartial observer might think, *Malvolio knows very well that Sir Toby does not like or respect him, but Maria is angry that Malvolio is going to tell Olivia that she served the late-night-partier Sir Toby a jug of wine, and so she exaggerates when she says that Malvolio "thinks that he is so crammed with excellent qualities that he believes with all his heart that all those who see him like him." If she is exaggerating about that, she may also be exaggerating about other things concerning Malvolio.*

Maria added, "I will exploit Malvolio's failings and make a fool of him."

Sir Toby asked, "What will you do?"

"I will drop where he will find it an ambiguous love letter that he will think is written to him because it will describe the color of his beard, the shape of his leg, the manner of his gait, the expression of his eye, his forehead, and his complexion. Malvolio shall read the letter and think that he is fully described in it. My handwriting is very similar to that of Olivia, your niece. When we find an old note that we have forgotten about, she and I can hardly decide which of us wrote it."

"Excellent! I smell an excellent practical joke," Sir Toby said

"I have it in my nose, too," Sir Andrew said.

"You will write a love letter and Malvolio shall find it," Sir Toby said. "He shall think that my niece wrote the letter and that she is in love with him."

"Yes," Maria said. "My idea is a horse of that color. If you had thought differently, that would be a horse of a different color."

Sir Andrew said, "Your horse of the same color is to make him an ass."

"You better believe it," Maria said.

"This is an admirable plan!" Sir Andrew said.

"It will be fun fit for a King," Maria said. "I know that my plan will work. He will get the medicine that is coming to him. You two and the fool will be placed where you can see Malvolio find and read the letter. You shall see how he interprets the letter and thinks that Olivia loves him. But right now, it is time to go to bed and dream about our joke and our revenge. Good night."

Maria exited.

Sir Toby said, "Good night, Penthesilea, Queen of the Amazons." This was another mild joke about Maria's short stature.

"I swear that she is a good woman," Sir Andrew said.

"She is a beagle — a small hound," Sir Toby said. "She adores me. What do you think about that?"

"I was adored once, too," Sir Andrew replied.

Men — and women — seek love. Using love as the bait for a trap was likely to work. And if Sir Andrew could be adored, why not Malvolio?

Sir Toby said, "It's time for bed, Sir Andrew. But remember to send for more money for us to spend."

"If I don't marry Olivia, your niece, I will be grievously out of pocket."

"Send for money, Sir Andrew. If you don't marry Olivia, then you have my permission to call me a eunuch."

"I do think that I will marry Olivia. If I don't, never again believe anything I say."

"Come with me," Sir Toby said. "I'll heat up some wine. It is too late to go to bed now. Come, Sir Andrew."

A drunk Sir Andrew was more likely to send away for more money.

Orsino, Viola, Orsino's attendant Curio, and others, including musicians, were in a room in Duke Orsino's palace.

Orsino said, "Play some music for me."

The musicians began to play.

Orsino said, "Good morning, friends. Cesario, remember that old and quaint song that we heard last night? I thought that it did relieve my lovesickness much more than the light airs and studied, artificial phrases of these fast and giddy-paced times. I would like to hear a verse of that song."

Curio answered, "The person is not here, sir, who should sing it."

"Who sings that song?"

"Feste, the jester, sir; he is a fool whom the lady Olivia's father took much delight in. He is somewhere in the palace."

"Find him, and while we wait we will listen to the music of that song."

Curio exited, and the musicians played the tune to the song. They had heard the song the previous night, and they knew the tune.

Orsino said to Viola, "Come here, young man. If you ever love someone, remember me as you endure its sweet pangs. For such as I am, all true lovers are: changeable and difficult to deal with. The only thing that I can focus on is the face of the woman I love."

He added, "Do you like this tune?"

Viola, who did like the tune, said, "It gives a very echo to the seat — the heart — where Love is throned. Anyone who hears it feels what a lover feels."

"You speak masterfully," Orsino said. "I swear that as young as you are, your eye has seen a face that it loves. Is that true, young man?"

"A little. Yes."

"What kind of woman do you love?"

"She is very much like you."

"In that case, you deserve someone better. How old is she?"

"About your age."

"Then she is too old," Orsino said. "A woman always ought to love someone who is older than she is. That way, she can adapt herself to him, and that way she will stay beautiful longer and keep herself in her husband's affection until that affection becomes rock-steady. After all, young man, although we men praise ourselves, we are not as constant in love as women are. Our loves are more giddy and unstable than the loves of women, and our loves are more flighty and wavering, and they are quicker to be lost and to become worn-out than the loves of women are."

"I think that you are right, sir," Viola said.

"So let the woman you love be younger than yourself, so you will continue to love her long enough for your love to become rock-steady. If she is older than you, she may lose her beauty too quickly for that to happen. Women are as roses, whose fair petals, once they have fully opened, do begin to fall to the ground that very hour."

"Unfortunately, the beauty of women is exactly like that," Viola said. "As soon as their beauty reaches perfection, it begins to die."

Curio returned with Feste. The musicians stopped playing.

Orsino said, "Feste, let me hear the song you sang last night. Listen to it, Cesario. It is old and plain. The spinners and the knitters in the sun and the carefree maidens who weave lace often sing it. It is simple truth, and its theme is the innocence of love in the old days."

Feste asked, "Are you ready to hear it, sir?"

"Yes. Please sing."

The musicians started playing, and Feste sang, "*Come quickly to me, come quickly, death,*

"*And in a sad coffin made of cypress let me be laid;*

"*Go away, go away, breath;*

"*I am slain by a fair cruel maiden.*

"*My shroud of white, adorned with yew leaves,*

"*Oh, prepare it!*

"*No lover more constant than I*

"*Has ever died for love.*

"*Not a flower, not a flower sweet*

"*On my black coffin let there be strewn;*

"*Not a friend, not a friend greet*

"*My poor corpse, where my bones shall be thrown:*

"*A thousand thousand sighs to save,*

"*Lay me, oh, where*

"Sad true lover shall never find my grave,

"To weep there!"

Feste thought, *The theme of this song is dying because of unrequited love. In the entire history of the world, this has never happened although many, many people have thought that it would happen. Right now, Orsino believes — or enjoys believing — that this could happen to him. He is wrong.*

Orsino gave Feste money, saying, "This is for your pains in singing that song."

"There is nothing painful about it, sir. I enjoy singing."

"In that case, the money is for your pleasure."

"As the saying goes," Feste said, "pleasure will be paid with pain, sooner or later."

"Give me now leave to leave thee," Orsino said. This was a polite way of saying that Feste should go now. Orsino was in a melancholy mood and not in a mood for jests.

Feste said, "May the melancholy god — Saturn — protect you; and may your tailor make your jacket out of iridescent silk because your changeable mind is like an opal that constantly changes colors. Men like you should become sea-merchants so that they could deal in everything and go everywhere. Your variable moods would match the variable moods of the sea. You would have a good sea voyage. Farewell."

Feste saw something in Orsino that made him think that Orsino was changeable, although so far Orsino had been consistent in expressing his love for Olivia. Certainly, Orsino had been changeable in one way. He had wanted to hear music, and so he had ordered Feste to be brought to him, but as soon as Feste had finished singing the song, Orsino had ordered him to go away.

Feste departed, and Orsino said, "Everyone except for Cesario, please leave."

They left, and Orsino said, "Once more, Cesario, go to Olivia, who cruelly does not love me, and tell this woman that my love is more noble than any other in the world. Tell her that I regard as lightly as fortune does her land and property and everything that she has inherited. Fortune does not value them, because it gives them and takes them away. What I value, and what attracts my soul, is the beauty with which nature has adorned Olivia."

Viola replied, "But what if she cannot love you, sir?"

"I will not take that for an answer."

"But you must, sir," Viola said. "Say that some lady — and such a lady may exist — loves you as much as you love Olivia. You cannot love this lady, and you tell her that. Doesn't she have to take that as an answer?"

"No woman's body could withstand the beating of so strong a passion as love has given to my heart. No woman's heart could be so big as to hold so much passion as my heart holds. Women lack the ability to retain such passion. Unfortunately, women's love is like appetite. It comes from the palate, not from the heart. Women's love can be more than satisfied — it can have too much and feel repulsion because of excess. But my appetite is as hungry as the sea. It can swallow everything. Make no comparison between the love that a woman could have for me and the love that I have for Olivia."

"Yes, but I know —"

"You know what?"

"I know too well how a woman can love a man. Truly, women are as true of heart as men. My father had a daughter who loved a man the way, perhaps, that I might love you, if I were a woman."

"What happened to her?"

"It is a blank page. She never told the man of her love for him, so her love stayed hidden. The concealment destroyed the rosiness of her cheeks like a worm destroys an apple. Brooding, she grieved with lovesickness, and with a pallid melancholy, she sat like a carving of smiling Patience on a tomb. She did not display the true emotion that she felt. Isn't this woman's behavior indicative of love? We men may say more and swear more, but indeed we are putting on a show. We men show greater love than we feel. We men make impressive vows of love, but the vows are more impressive than the love."

"Did your sister die of love?"

"I am all the daughters of my father's house, and all the brothers too, but as of now I do not know the answer to that question," Viola said.

She asked, "Shall I go and see Olivia for you?"

"Yes. That is the business at hand. Go quickly to her. Give her this jewel and tell her my love for her cannot be restrained and that she must love me."

A change had been made in Maria's plan. She would still plant the forged love letter where Malvolio would find it, but the people who would witness what would happen afterward would be Sir Toby, Sir Andrew, and Fabian, a servant who knew Sir Toby well and was on good terms with him. Fabian did not work directly under Malvolio. The original plan had been for Feste, not Fabian, to be present when Malvolio found the forged letter.

Sir Toby, Sir Andrew, and Fabian were in Olivia's garden, a place where Malvolio liked to take walks.

Sir Toby said, "Come with us, Mr. Fabian."

"Absolutely," Fabian said. "I do not want to miss this. If I did, I would drown in sadness."

Sir Toby asked Fabian, "Won't you be happy to see this sheep-biter, this sneaky dog, this hypocrite, this Malvolio be shamed?"

"I would exult. Did you know that he got me into trouble with Olivia because of a bear-baiting here? Olivia is tender-hearted and does not want bears to be chained up and then attacked by dogs."

Sir Toby said, "To make Malvolio angry, we will bring the bear back here, and we will fool Malvolio so badly that he will feel as if he is black and blue with bruises. Isn't that right, Sir Andrew?"

"It certainly is. If we don't make a fool of Malvolio, we don't deserve to live."

Sir Toby saw Maria coming toward them and said, "Here comes the little practical joker."

Maria told the three men, "All of you hide yourselves in the shrubbery. Malvolio is coming this way. For the past half-hour, he has been walking in the sunlight and using his shadow as a mirror as he practices courtly gestures. Watch him, and laugh at him. I know that this letter I forged will make a self-deceiving idiot of him. Hide, if you want to have a good laugh."

She dropped the letter on the ground and said, "Lie there until Malvolio finds you. Poachers catch trout by stroking their gills. We will catch Malvolio by stroking his ego with flattery. His pride will make him believe that this letter proves that Olivia loves him."

Maria departed, and Malvolio arrived.

Malvolio said to himself, "Luck is important. Luck is all-important. I am not married to Olivia because of bad luck. I had the bad luck to be born into a lower social class than Olivia. Maria once told me that Olivia was fond of me, and I have heard Olivia herself come close to saying she loved me. She said that, if she ever fell in love, it would be with someone who is like me. In addition, she treats me better and with more respect than she does any of her other servants. Knowing these things, what should I think?"

"He's an overweening, arrogant, presumptuous rogue!" Sir Toby said.

"Be quiet!" Fabian said. "His conceit is making a proud rooster out of him. Look at how he struts with his nose held high!"

"I could so beat the rogue!" Sir Andrew said.

"Be quiet, I say!" Sir Toby said.

Malvolio said, "I want to be Count Malvolio!"

"Idiot!" Sir Toby said.

"Shoot him!" Sir Andrew said.

"Be quiet," Sir Toby said.

"I could be Count Malvolio. There is precedent for it. A woman from a high social class married a man from a lower social class: The lady of the Strachy married the yeoman of the wardrobe."

"Damn him! He is like Jezebel, the proud wife in the Old Testament!" Sir Andrew said.

"Shh!" Fabian whispered. "Malvolio is deep in his daydream. His imagination is making him swell up his chest."

"After I have been married to Olivia for three months, and after I have sat in my chair of state — my throne — for three months —"

"I would like to have a crossbow that can fire stones right now," Sir Toby said. "I would hit him in the eye!"

Malvolio continued, "I would call my servants together, as I wore my velvet robe that is embroidered with leafy branches. I would have just come from a couch where I left Olivia sleeping."

Presumably, she would be sleeping after a session of sex.

"Fire and brimstone!" Sir Toby said.

"Shh!" Fabian hissed.

"I would adopt an air of authority, and I would gravely look at all who are present and tell them that I know my place and I hope that they know their place. Then I would ask for my new relative Sir Toby."

"Bring bolts and shackles! Bring fetters!" Sir Toby said.

"Shh! Be quiet!" Fabian said.

"Seven of my servants would obediently go out to find Sir Toby," Malvolio said. "I would frown as I wait. Perhaps I would wind my watch or I would play with my —"

Here Malvolio touched the chain that stewards wore as a mark of their position. He remembered that if he married Olivia he would no longer wear a chain, and so he finished the sentence with "some rich jewel."

Neglecting to say "Sir," he continued, "Toby approaches and bows to me."

"I am going to kill this guy," Sir Toby said.

"Although it is torture, we must be quiet," Fabian said.

Malvolio continued, "I would extend my hand to him like this, and I would replace my friendly smile with a stern look of authority."

Sir Toby said, "And then I would hit him in the mouth."

Malvolio continued, "I then say, 'Kinsman Toby, my having married your niece gives me the right to speak to you frankly.'"

"Oh, really?" Sir Toby said.

Malvolio continued, "You must stop getting drunk."

"And you must stop being a jackass," Sir Toby said.

"Be quiet," Fabian said, "or you will ruin our trap."

Malvolio continued, "In addition, you are wasting your time with a foolish knight."

Sir Andrew said, "He means me. I'm sure of it."

Malvolio continued, "I refer, of course, to Sir Andrew."

Sir Andrew said, "I knew that he meant me. Lots of people call me foolish."

Malvolio saw the letter that Maria had written and then dropped in the garden. He said, "What is this?"

Fabian said, "The mouse has seen the cheese in the trap."

Malvolio picked up the letter.

Sir Toby said, "Shh! Please, please, read the letter out loud!"

Malvolio looked at the writing on the outside of the letter and said, "This is Olivia's handwriting. Look! Here are her exact C's, her U's and her T's and this is how she makes her big P's. It is, without any question, her handwriting."

Sir Andrew asked, "Why 'seas,' 'ewes,' and 'teas'?"

Sir Toby and Fabian both smiled, knowing as they did that CUT was a slang expression for a vulva and knowing as they did that vulvas are useful in making big pees.

As Sir Toby had hoped, Malvolio began to read the letter out loud: "*To the unknown beloved, this letter, and my good wishes.*"

Malvolio said, "These are the exact phrases that she uses while writing."

He looked at the sealing wax and saw the picture of Lucrece, a Roman woman who had committed suicide after being raped by an Etruscan King's son, imprinted in the wax. The Italians then overthrew the Etruscan King and established the Roman Republic.

Malvolio said, "This is more proof that Olivia wrote this letter. It is sealed with her seal. But to whom is this letter written?"

Fabian said, "He will take the bait — and he will take it hook, line, and sinker."

Malvolio read out loud, "*Jove knows I love:*

"*But who?*

"*Lips, do not move;*

"*No man must know.*"

Malvolio said, "'*No man must know.*' What follows this line? The meter of poetry now changes! I wonder if Olivia is referring to me."

"Hang yourself now, you stinking badger," Sir Toby said.

Malvolio read out loud, "*I may command where I adore;*

"*But silence, like the knife of Lucrece,*

"*With bloodless stroke my heart does gore:*

"*M, O, A, I does rule my life.*"

Fabian said, "This riddle uses ridiculously lofty language!"

"Maria is an excellent woman, I believe," Sir Toby said.

Malvolio said, "'*M, O, A, I does rule my life.*' Hmm, let's think about this."

Fabian said, "Maria has mixed a drink of poison for him."

"And he is eager to drink it," Sir Toby said.

Malvolio said, "'*I may command where I adore.*' Why, Olivia may command me. I am her servant. She is the lady who gives me orders. Why, the meaning of the sentence is obvious to any reasonable mind. There is no difficulty in understanding the meaning of this sentence."

He looked at the letter and said, "What about the end: '*M, O, A, I does rule my life*'? Here is an alphabetical puzzle. What is its meaning? If only these letters related to me! Think! M, O, A, I."

Sir Toby said, "Malvolio is like a hunting dog trying to find a scent. But the scent is cold."

Fabian said, "The dog will find the scent again and howl as if it has made a great discovery. Malvolio will follow the false scent, although the true scent actually stinks like a fox and Malvolio should be able to easily find it."

Malvolio said, "M. Malvolio. M is the first letter of my name!"

Fabian said, "Didn't I say that he would find the false scent again? He is good at picking up scents."

Malvolio said, "That explains M. But there is no consistent explanation of the following letters. A should be the next letter, but O is the letter that actually follows M."

Fabian said, "And O shall be Malvolio's end, I hope. Let an O — a hangman's noose — be around his neck."

"Aye, or I'll beat him," Sir Toby said, "and make him cry, 'Oh!'"

Malvolio said, "M, O, A, I. An 'I' comes at the end."

Fabian said, "Aye. If you had an eye in the back of your head, you might see more detraction and loss of reputation at your heels than good fortune in front of you."

Malvolio said, "M, O, A, I: This puzzle is not like the former puzzle, and yet, I can make it solvable — all of these letters are in my name. But there is more. At this point, the letter contains prose."

Malvolio read out loud, "*If this letter should fall into your hands, think. In my good fortune I am above you in social class; but be not afraid of greatness: some are born great, some achieve greatness, and some have greatness thrust upon them. Your Fates have generously opened their hands; let your passion and courage embrace them. And, to accustom yourself to what you are likely to be, cast off your humble ways and appear fresh and new. Be disagreeable with a kinsman, be surly with servants; let your tongue speak about important matters; make yourself act eccentrically. Thus the woman who sighs with love for you advises you. Remember who complimented your yellow stockings, and who wished to see you wearing garters that cross your leg. Remember, I say. Do these things. Your fortune is made — if you want it to be made. If you do not, do everything the way that you have always done them and make no change in your life. Go ahead and stay a steward, be a companion to servants, and show that you are not worthy to touch the fingers of Fortune. Farewell from a woman who now commands you but would like you to command her. THE FORTUNATE UNHAPPY."*

Malvolio paused and then said, "Everything is clear. Daylight and open country cannot reveal anything more. The meaning of this letter is straightforward, and I will do as it says. I will be proud, I will read authors who write about politics, I will treat Sir Toby with contempt, and I will stop being the companions of servants; in short, I will do everything to the letter that this letter tells me to do."

He added, "I do not now fool myself. I am not letting my imagination deceive me. Everything points to this conclusion: Olivia loves me. She did compliment my yellow stockings recently, and she did praise my legs when they were cross-gartered. In this letter, she declares her love for me, and she tells me how she wishes me to act. I thank my good fortune. I am happy. I will do as she wishes. I will immediately be distant and aloof and proud. I will dress in yellow stockings and be cross-gartered, just as quickly as I can change my clothing. Jove and good fortune be praised!"

He looked at the letter and said, "Here is a postscript: 'You must know who I am. If you accept my love, show it by smiling. Your smiles are becoming; therefore, please smile whenever you are in my presence, my sweet dear.'"

Malvolio added, "Jove, I thank you. I will smile. I will do everything that Olivia will have me do."

Malvolio left the garden.

An impartial observer — and everyone else — might think, *Malvolio did not correctly solve the puzzle of M, O, A, I. True enough. But what is the correct solution to the puzzle? What if M, O, A, and I are — in part — an anagram? We certainly have seen Malvolio and the people spying on him when he finds the letter in Olivia's garden talk about rearranging the letters. Malvolio tells us that A should go after M, and Fabian mentions O and end. What do we get when we rearrange the letters and put I at the beginning? I M A O. I am A and O.*

The O goes at the end, and the end is Omega. If the end is Omega, what is the beginning? The beginning is Alpha. Therefore, I am Alpha and Omega. This is Revelation 22:13: "I am Alpha and Omega, the beginning and the end, the first and the last." These are words — and letters — that apply to God, but Malvolio is applying them to himself. Revelation is the last book of the Bible. What is the first book of the Bible? Genesis. What is the most important part of Genesis? The Fall. The serpent tempted Eve to eat the fruit of the Tree of Knowledge of Good and Evil: "For God doth know that in the day ye eat thereof, then your eyes shall be opened, and ye shall be as gods, knowing good and evil." Eve — and Adam — ate the fruit, committing the sin of pride. They placed themselves before God and disobeyed the command of God. The sin of pride is regarding oneself as the center of the universe, as being more important than anything or anybody else. Pride is a deadly sin, and it is the foundation of the other deadly sins:

1) Pride.

I am the center of the universe, and I am better than other people. Quite simply, I am more important than other people.

2) Envy.

I am the center of the universe, so I ought to have it all, and if you have something I want, I envy you.

3) Wrath.

Because I am the center of the universe, everything ought to go my way, and when it does not, I get angry.

4) Sloth.

I am the center of the universe, so I don't have to work at something. Either other people can do my work for me, or they can give me credit for work I have not done because if I had done the work, I would have done it excellently.

5) Avariciousness and Prodigality.

I am the center of the universe, so I deserve to have what I want. If I want money, I get money and never spend it, or if I want the things that money can buy, then I spend every dime I can make or borrow to get what I want. Either way, I deserve to have what I want.

6) Gluttony.

I am the center of the universe, so I deserve these two extra pieces of pie every night. This is my reward to myself for being so fabulous.

7) Lust.

I am the center of the universe, so my needs take precedence over the needs of everyone else. If I want to get laid, it's OK if I lie to get someone in bed and never call in the days and weeks afterward. My sexual pleasure is more important than the hurt of someone who realizes that he or she has been used.

Malvolio's name is Mal Volio — "I wish badly." Proud people wish badly.

The rebellion of Adam and Eve in the Garden of Eden led to the first sin committed by human beings. Previously, an angel had committed the first sin by supernatural beings.

That proud supernatural being is Lucifer, who put himself before God and rebelled against him. Because of this sin, Lucifer is condemned to spend eternity shackled in the darkness of Hell. Adam and Eve committed the original sin of human beings. Lucifer committed the original sin of supernatural beings.

If Malvolio were a better person, he would solve the puzzle of I M A O correctly and he would realize that he is guilty of the sin of pride. He wants to marry Olivia, but he wants to marry her because doing so will improve his position in society. He does not want to marry Olivia because he can make her happy. He loves Olivia's social standing and her wealth.

Malvolio regards himself as being more important than Olivia: I am the center of the universe, and I ought to marry Olivia because doing so will make ME happy. I am the center of the universe, and I ought to marry Olivia for her social standing and money. I am the center of the universe, and I ought to marry Olivia although I do not love her.

If Malvolio were a more intelligent person, he would realize that he on the verge of a fall just like Adam and Eve were when the serpent tempted them in the Garden of Eden or like Lucifer when he rebelled against God.

Malvolio is not morally good enough or intelligent enough to correctly solve Maria's puzzle. He believes the letter that Maria wrote and he will be punished for believing it just like Lucifer was punished. However, the people judging him and punishing him are not God.

Maria and the others spying on Malvolio are also guilty of pride. They consider themselves better than Malvolio. They consider the entertainment they will get by watching Malvolio being manipulated into making a fool of himself is more valuable than Malvolio's future hurt feelings.

Fabian watched Malvolio walk away, and then he said, "I would not have missed this entertainment even if the Shah of Persia had offered me a pension of thousands of pounds."

"I could marry Maria as a reward for this practical joke," Sir Toby said.

Sir Andrew, who sometimes repeated whatever Sir Toby said, being incapable sometimes of figuring out something to say, said, "I could marry her, too."

Sir Toby said, "I would not even ask her for a dowry — except for another practical joke like this one."

"Me, too," Sir Andrew said.

Fabian said, "Here comes the trickster herself."

Maria walked up to the three men.

Sir Toby asked, "May I kiss your feet?"

"May I, also?" Sir Andrew asked.

Sir Toby asked, "Would you like me to be your servant for the rest of my life?"

"And would you like me to be your lifelong servant?" Sir Andrew asked.

Sir Toby said, "Your practical joke has worked so well that Malvolio is living in a dream. When his bubble of a daydream bursts, he will go mad."

"Tell me the truth," Maria said. "Did my letter really work?"

"He took to the letter like a midwife takes to brandy," Sir Toby said.

"If you want to see how the practical joke will work out," Maria said, "watch Malvolio the next time he appears before Olivia. He will wear yellow stockings, and yellow is a color she hates. He will be cross-gartered, and that is a style she hates. He will smile constantly, and she will dislike that because she is now in a mood for melancholy. Malvolio will definitely make a fool of himself in front of her. If you wish to witness this, follow me."

Earlier, Malvolio had said about Olivia, "She did compliment my yellow stockings recently, and she did praise my legs when they were cross-gartered."

Possibly, Maria is lying about Olivia dislikes.

"I will follow you to the gates of Hell, you most excellent Devil of wit," Sir Toby said.

"I'll go, too," Sir Andrew said.

They followed Maria into Olivia's house.

CHAPTER 3

— 3.1 —

A little later, Viola walked into Olivia's garden, where she met Feste, who had a small drum — known as a tabor —hanging around his neck.

"God bless you and your music, friend," Viola said. "Do you live by your drum?"

Feste replied, "No, sir, I live by the church."

"Are you a member of the clergy?"

"No, sir, but I live by the church; for I live at my house, and my house stands by the church."

"When I asked, 'Do you live by your drum?' I meant, 'Do you make your living by playing your drum?' I see that you are playing with language. You would say that the King lies by a beggar if a beggar dwells near him. But then you would make 'lies by the beggar' mean 'sleeps with the beggar.' Or you would say that the church stands by your drum, if the church is standing by — that is, located next to — your drum. But then you would have 'stands by' mean the church 'is supported by' your drum if you donate to the church some of the money your playing the drum earns for you. Or you would have 'stands by' mean the church 'is supported by' your drum if your drum leans against the church."

"Well said, sir," Feste replied. "We live in a wonderful age. A sentence is like a glove to a good wit. A good wit can turn a sentence inside out as easily as he can turn a glove inside out."

"That's the truth," Viola said. "People who play with words can quickly make them wanton and undisciplined."

"That's why I wish that my sister had no name, sir," Feste replied.

"Why is that?"

"Why, sir, her name is a word; and to play with that word might make my sister wanton. But indeed words are very untrustworthy now that they are used in legal documents."

"Why can't the words in legal documents be relied on?" Viola asked.

"To tell the truth, in order to answer your question I would have to use words, and words are so wanton and undisciplined that I am loath to try to talk sense with them," Feste said.

"I believe that you are a merry fellow and care for nothing. You are carefree, and you don't care what you say."

"That's not true," Feste said. "I do care for something. I care for Olivia. In my heart, I do not care for you. If that means that I do not care for nothing, sir, then you should disappear because you are nothing to me. If you are bringing another unwelcome message from Orsino to Olivia, it would be best if you left."

Viola had no intention of leaving, but she realized that Feste was witty.

"I think I recognize you now," Viola said, "Aren't you the Lady Olivia's fool?"

"No, indeed not, sir," Feste replied. "The Lady Olivia has no folly. She will keep no fool, sir, until she is married. Fools are to husbands as oranges are to grapefruits; the husband is bigger and makes the bigger fool. Indeed, I am not Olivia's fool — I am her corrupter of words."

"I saw you recently at the palace of Duke Orsino."

"Foolery, sir, walks around the world like the Sun does. Foolery and the Sun shine everywhere. Shouldn't Orsino's fool be with him as much as I am with Olivia? I think I saw your wisdom at the palace of Duke Orsino."

"Whoa!" Viola said. "If you are going to call me a fool, I will have no more to do with you. Wait. Here is a coin for you."

Feste took the coin and said, "The next time Jove receives a delivery of hair, may he give you a beard."

"To tell the truth, I am almost sick because I don't have a beard," Olivia replied.

That's true, she thought. *I love and want Orsino, and he has a beard. I certainly don't want a beard that grows on* my *chin.*

She asked Feste, "Is Olivia inside?"

He held out the coin and said, "Would not a pair of these breed, sir?"

"They would, indeed, if kept together and invested wisely."

"I would like to play Lord Pandarus of Phrygia, sir, and introduce this coin, whose name is Troilus, sir, to a coin named Cressida."

Troilus and Cressida were two Trojans who had had a famous love affair with Pandarus as their go-between.

Viola gave him a second coin and said, "I understand you, sir. It is well begged. Here is a female coin to go with the male coin I gave you earlier."

Earlier, Feste had made a jab at Viola when he said that he did not care for her. Now, Viola returned the jab by calling Feste a beggar. (Professional fools are not beggars, even when they jest for tips.) Tit for tat, and Feste respected that — but he would make it clear that Cressida, and not he — was a beggar.

"I hope that my request for a second coin is not a big deal, sir," Feste said, "Begging for a beggar is not wrong. It is said that Cressida became a beggar in her old age."

A beggar's begging is not wrong. It is the beggar's vocation, and it is no sin to labor in one's vocation.

Feste added, "To answer your question, Olivia is inside the house. I will tell the people inside that you are here and from where you have come. Who you are and why you have come is not part of what I know. I would say that I'm out of my element, but that's a cliché."

Feste left to tell Olivia that a young man wanted to talk to her.

Viola respected Feste's wit, but she was loyal to Orsino. Feste respected Viola's wit, but he was loyal to Olivia.

She said to herself about Feste, "This fellow is wise enough to play the fool; and to do that well requires a kind of wit. He must observe the mood of those with whom he jests. He must observe their social standing and the occasion. He can't be like a hungry hawk that seizes every opportunity to hunt; instead, Feste must seize every *proper* opportunity to get what he wants, which means that he must know when and when not to make a joke. His is a skill as full of labor as the art of a wise man. A fool's folly is full of wit and wisdom, but a wise man who falls into folly loses his reputation for wit and wisdom."

Viola also thought about Feste calling her a fool. Normally, that is an insult, but when a professional fool — a wise fool — calls you a fool, and even refers to you as "your wisdom," perhaps it ought to be regarded as a compliment.

Sir Toby and Sir Andrew walked up to Viola.

"God bless you, gentleman," Sir Toby said to Viola.

She replied, "And you, sir."

Sir Andrew said to her, "*Dieu vous garde, monsieur,*" which is French for "God keep you, sir."

Viola replied, "*Et vous aussi; votre serviteur,*" which is French for "And you, too; at your service."

Sir Andrew, who did not know French well, replied, "I hope, sir, you are; and I am yours."

Sir Toby's language could be odd. He said to Viola, "Will you encounter the house? My niece is desirous that you should enter, if your business is with her."

Viola replied, "I am bound for your niece, sir. She is the list — the destination — of my voyage."

"Taste your legs, sir; put them to motion," Sir Toby said.

"My legs do better understand me, sir — they stand under me — than I understand what you mean by bidding me to 'taste' my legs," Viola replied.

"I mean, to go, sir, to enter," Sir Toby said.

I understand now, Viola thought. *"Taste" is a word for the verb "test." I have heard of tasting valor, but I have never before now heard of tasting legs. Also, Sir Toby made a malapropism when he said "encounter" rather than "enter." Another way for words to be unmanageable is for them to be misused. Sir Toby is trying to be fancy in his word choice, and he is making mistakes. Yet another way for words to be unmanageable is when someone does not understand a language well.*

She replied, "I would answer you with gait and entrance, but we are forestalled. I see Olivia and Maria walking toward us."

Viola said to Olivia, "Most excellent accomplished lady, may the Heavens rain perfume on you!"

Sir Andrew appreciated Viola's choice of words. He said to himself, "'Rain perfume' — well said."

Viola said to Olivia, "My message is for only your receptive and attentive ears."

Sir Andrew said to himself, "'Rain perfume,' 'receptive,' and 'attentive' — I intend to memorize all three and have them ready to use in conversation."

Olivia said, "Leave me and this young man alone, and shut the door to the garden."

Sir Toby, Sir Andrew, and Maria all left, leaving Viola and Olivia alone in the garden.

Olivia said to Viola, "Give me your hand, sir."

Viola gave Olivia her hand, and she bowed and then let go of Olivia's hand.

Viola said, "I give you my duty, madam, and my most humble service."

"What is your name?"

"Cesario is my name, and I am your servant, fair princess."

"You are my servant! The world has never been happy ever since fake humility was called flattery. You are Duke Orsino's servant, young man."

"Count Orsino is your servant, and therefore what is his is yours. Your servant's servant is your servant, madam."

"As for Duke Orsino, I never think about him. As for his thoughts, I wish that they were blank rather than filled with me."

"Madam, I have come to urge you to like him."

"Please, I beg you to never speak again about him to me. However, if you would like to undertake another suit — your own — I had rather hear you do that than to hear the music from the spheres."

According to the medieval conception of the universe, t the center of the universe is the Earth, but nine spheres surround it: the seven spheres of seven planets, the sphere of the firmament, and then the Primum Mobile, which imparts motion to the other spheres. The firmament is where the constellations and fixed stars are embedded. (Mercury, Venus, Mars, Jupiter, and Saturn are called "wandering stars" or "erring stars" because they wander in the sky; the word "planet" comes from a Greek term and means "wandering star." One meaning of "err" is "wander.") When the crystalline spheres move, they create music.

Viola was shocked: "Dear lady!"

"Let me speak, please. After you first visited me — and enchanted me — I sent a servant after you to give you a ring. Thus did I wrong myself, my servant, and, I fear, you. I wronged myself by lying, I wronged my servant, Malvolio, by making him lie, and I wronged you by implying that you had thrown the ring at me. You must have a harsh interpretation of my deed and of myself because I tried to force the ring on you with shameful cunning. You knew that the ring did not belong to you. What must you think?

"Haven't you been setting me and my honor at the stake like a bear and tormenting me? Haven't you been cruelly laughing at me for my so passionate actions? I have revealed enough of myself to you that you, with your intelligence and perception, understand me. Only a thin piece of gauze covers my heart, which I know that you can see. So, let me hear you speak."

Viola, who knew that Olivia was passionately in love with her, said, "I pity you." She also put Olivia's ring on a piece of furniture.

Olivia replied, "Pity is a step toward love."

"No, it is not a step toward love," Viola replied. "It is common knowledge that often we pity our enemies."

"Well, then I can smile again because my enemy shows me pity," Olivia said. "How proud the poor are! The poor and the deprived such as myself are so quick to grasp at straws that might bring them a little happiness! If one should be a prey, how much better it is to fall before the lion than the wolf! In other words, although you do not love me, at least I fell in love with a man who is worthy to be loved. I have been destroyed by a noble enemy rather than an ignoble one."

Olivia also thought, *You, Cesario, are only a servant and I am a Countess, but you show that you are proud by rejecting my love for you.*

The clock struck.

Olivia said, "The clock criticizes me for wasting time. Do not be afraid, young man — I cannot force you to marry me. However, when your wit and youth have arrived at maturity, your wife is likely to reap a proper man."

Olivia pointed to the garden gate and said, "There lies your way, due west."

"Then westward-ho!" Viola replied. "May God bless you and give peace of mind to you."

She added, "Do you have a message for me to take to Orsino?"

Olivia did not speak, and Viola turned to go.

"Wait," Olivia said. "Please, tell me what you think of me."

"I think that you do think you are not what you are," Viola said.

This sentence is ambiguous. Viola meant this: *You do not think that you are in love with a woman, but you are.*

Olivia, however, understood the sentence to mean this: *You do not think that you are behaving beneath your social class — you are a Countess who is in love with a gentleman servant — but you are.*

Olivia replied, "If I think so, I think the same of you."

By this, she meant that she believed that Viola was of a higher social class than she was pretending to be.

This was true. As Cesario, of course, Viola was working as a gentleman servant, but she was born into a higher class.

Viola said, "Then know that you think rightly: I am not what I am."

Viola meant that yes, she was not what she was pretending to be. She meant that she was a woman pretending to be a man, but Olivia thought that Viola was talking about social class.

Olivia said, "I would you were as I would have you be!"

She meant this: *I wish that you would return my love!*

Viola replied, "Would that be an improvement? I wish that it would be. Right now I am your fool. You are wasting my time. You told me to leave, and then you told me to stay. You are treating me as if I were your fool. I must obey you because I represent Orsino and he would not want me to be rude to you and leave."

Olivia thought, *Cesario looks beautiful when he's angry and scornful! His lips show his anger and contempt! He is showing that he is angry at me, but that increases my love for him. Guilt due to murder cannot conceal itself, and neither can love. Love's night is noon. Love tries to hide itself, but it is as obvious as the noon Sun. I have made Cesario angry, but even now I cannot conceal my love for him.*

Olivia said to Viola, "Cesario, by the roses of the spring, by virginity, honor, truth, and everything, I love you so much that despite all your pride — and you show your pride by rejecting me — neither my intelligence nor my reason can hide my passion for you. Don't think that you ought not to love me because I have pursued you. Instead, reason this way: Love sought is good, but love given unsought is better."

Viola replied, "I swear by my innocence and by my youth that I have one heart, one bosom, and one truth, and that no woman has ever been or ever will be mistress of it, except for me. And so goodbye, good madam. I will never again bring to you Orsino's tearful love messages that so deplore you."

"Please come here again," Olivia said. "Perhaps you may move a heart, which now hates, to like his love."

Olivia was deliberately ambiguous, hoping that Viola would misunderstand what she had said.

She hoped that Viola would think that she had meant this: *Perhaps you may move my heart, which now hates Orsino, to like his love for me.*

But Olivia actually meant this: *Perhaps you may move your own heart, which now hates me, to like Orsino's love, who is me.*

Sir Toby, Sir Andrew, and Fabian were meeting in a room in Olivia's house.

Sir Andrew, who was angry, said, "No, I will not stay in this house a second longer."

"Your reason, dear venomous one," Sir Toby said, "give us your reason."

Fabian said, "Yes, you must tell us your reason."

Sir Andrew said to Sir Toby, "I saw your niece treating Duke Orsino's young messenger much better than she has ever treated me. I saw them together in the garden."

Sir Toby asked, "Did my niece see you looking at her and Duke Orsino's young messenger?"

"She saw me as plainly as I see you now," Sir Andrew replied.

Fabian, who was as eager and willing as Sir Toby to make a fool of Sir Andrew by playing a trick on him, said, "This is evidence that Olivia loves you."

"Are you trying to make a fool of me?" Sir Andrew asked.

"I can prove that Olivia loves you by using judgment and reason," Fabian said.

Fabian did not mention truth.

Sir Toby said to Sir Andrew, "Judgment and reason have been part of the grand jury since before Noah was a sailor."

Fabian said, "Olivia showed favor to Orsino's young messenger in your sight only to make you jealous, to exasperate you, to awaken your sleeping valor, to put fire in your heart and brimstone in your passion. You should then have accosted her; and with some excellent jests, as brilliant as coins fresh from the mint, you should have made the youth speechless. She wanted you to do that, but you did not. You have wasted a golden opportunity. Now you have sailed into the north of Olivia's regard, and she regards you frostily, as if you were hanging like an icicle on a Dutchman's beard, unless you redeem yourself by doing some praiseworthy deed either of bravery or cunning."

Sir Andrew replied, "If it must be done, it must be done with a brave act because I hate cunning. I would rather be a heretic than a cunning schemer."

"Why, then build your fortunes upon the basis of bravery," Sir Toby said. "Challenge Orsino's young messenger to a fight. Wound him in eleven places.

My niece shall take note of it; assure yourself that nothing in the world is better than a report of valor in getting a woman to love you."

Fabian said, "There is no other way to proceed than this, Sir Andrew."

"Will either of you carry my challenge to Orsino's young messenger?"

"Go and write your challenge in a martial hand," Sir Toby said. "Be fierce and brief. Your letter does not need to be cunning, but it ought to be eloquent and filled with lies. Talk down to him and insult him. Write as many lies as will lie in your paper, no matter how big the sheet of paper is. Even if your paper is about three meters square — as big as a sheet that fits the bed of Ware in England — fill it with lies. Although you write with the pen of a goose — one made from a goose feather — let your ink be mixed with gall."

Sir Toby thought, *Yes, Sir Andrew will be writing with the pen of a goose — he is a goose.*

"Where shall I find you after I have written the challenge?"

Sir Toby replied, "We will call on you in your bed-chamber. Go now and write."

Sir Andrew left to write his challenge.

Fabian said, "He is a dear puppet to you, Sir Toby. You can manipulate him so easily."

"I have been dear — expensive — to him, lad," Sir Toby said. "I have spent approximately two thousand of his ducats. His income is three thousand ducats per year."

"The letter he writes will be remarkable. Are you actually thinking of delivering the letter to Orsino's young messenger?"

Fabian thought, *We don't want to carry the joke too far.*

"Of course I will," Sir Toby said. "If I don't, never again believe a word I say. In the meantime, find Orsino's young messenger and do whatever you can to make him ready to fight Sir Andrew. I think that oxen and heavy ropes will not be able to get Sir Andrew and the young messenger together so that they can fight. If you ever see Sir Andrew shirtless, look at his back. If he doesn't have a yellow streak there, I swear that I will become a cannibal."

Fabian said, "Sir Andrew's opponent, the young messenger, bears in his face no sign of fierceness. He does not look like a fighter."

Maria walked up to Sir Toby and Fabian.

Sir Toby said to Fabian, "Look, the youngest wren of nine is walking toward us."

He was commenting on Maria's small size. According to folklore, the smallest bird hatches last.

Maria said to them, "If you want to laugh so hard that you will have stitches in your side, come with me. The fool Malvolio has become a heathen and renounced Christianity. No one who wants to be saved by believing the right things could ever believe the absurdities that I put in my letter — and act them out! He is doing everything that my letter told him to do. He is wearing yellow stockings."

"Is he cross-gartered?" Sir Toby asked.

"Yes, he is, and that style looks abominable," Maria said. "He looks like a pedant who keeps a school in the church. He thinks that he looks stylish, but he looks old-fashioned and rustic and obsolete. I have dogged him — I have followed him as if I were his murderer and were going to ambush him. He is obeying every point of the letter that I dropped to betray him. He smiles his face into more lines than is in a new map with the newest island created by underwater volcanoes. You have never seen such a funny sight as his smiling face. I can hardly keep myself from throwing things at him. I know that Olivia will hit him. If she does, he will smile and think that she likes him."

Sir Toby said, "Lead us to where Malvolio is."

On a street in a town in Illyria, Sebastian and Antonio were talking.

Sebastian said, "I did not want to trouble you, but since you enjoy helping me, I will no longer nag you to stop."

"I could not stay behind and let you travel alone," Antonio said. "My desire, which is sharper than the point of a steel spur, spurred me on to follow and find you. I did not want just to see you, although that desire would have made me take an even longer voyage. Instead, I was worried about what might happen to you during your travels. You do not know this territory, which can be rough and inhospitable to an unguided and friendless stranger. My deep friendship for you, reinforced by my fear of what might happen to you, led me to set forth and follow you."

"My kind Antonio," Sebastian said, "I can make no other answer but thanks, and thanks, and thanks again. All too often good deeds are thanked with words and not money, but if my wealth were as great as my sense of gratitude to you, you would receive better treatment than I can now give you."

He added, "What shall we do now? Shall we go and see the sights of this town?"

"Let us do that tomorrow, sir," Antonio said. "It is best to first go and see about our lodging."

"I am not tired, and it is a long time until night. Please, let us satisfy our eyes with the memorials and the things of fame that make this town renowned."

"Please pardon me," Antonio said. "I do not without danger walk these streets. Once, in a sea-fight, I fought against Duke Orsino's galleys and did such deeds of note that if I were arrested here, I would be in serious trouble."

"Do you kill a great number of his people?"

"No," Antonio said. "That did not happen, although the time and reason of the quarrel could have led to great bloodshed. This quarrel could have been patched up by now. All that was needed to do was to return to Duke Orsino's people what we had taken from them. In fact, most of us did that because we wanted to be able to do business with Illyria. I alone did not return what I had taken. Because of that, if I am arrested in Illyria, I shall pay a heavy price."

"Don't be conspicuous in this country."

"I don't intend to be," Antonio said. "Wait, Sebastian, here is my wallet and money. The best place to lodge in this town is in the south suburbs at the Elephant Inn. You go ahead and take in the sights here and learn about the town; I will go to the Elephant and order our meals and arrange for our lodging. You will find me at the Elephant."

"Why did you give me your wallet and money to hold for you?"

"Perhaps as you are wandering the town, you will see some trifle that you would like to buy. Your own money is not sufficient, I think, for unnecessary purchases."

"I will be your money-bearer and leave you for an hour."

"I will be at the Elephant Inn."

"I will meet you there."

— 3.4 —

Olivia and Maria talked together in Olivia's garden.

Olivia said to herself, "I have sent a servant after Orsino's young messenger, Cesario, to make him come back and see me. What kind of food should I serve him? What gift should I give him? Young men are bought — won over with gifts — more often than begged or borrowed."

She noticed Maria looking at her, and then she said to herself, "I am too loud."

She said in her normal voice to Maria, "Where is Malvolio? He is serious and respectable, and he is well suited to be a servant to me now."

She thought, *Right now, I am hopelessly in love with someone who does not love me.*

She asked again, "Where is Malvolio?"

"He is coming, madam, but he is behaving very strangely," Maria replied. "He seems to be possessed by the Devil, madam."

"Why, what's the matter with him? Does he rave?"

"No, madam, he does nothing but smile. I advise that your ladyship have a bodyguard near you when Malvolio comes. I am sure that the man's wits are tainted."

"Go and tell him to come here."

Maria exited.

Olivia said to herself, "I am as mad — as insane — as he is, if sad madness and merry madness are equally madness. Malvolio does nothing but smile, as his is a merry madness. I cannot smile, as mine is a sad madness."

Maria and Malvolio walked into the garden.

Olivia asked Malvolio, who was indeed smiling, and who continued to smile, "How are you, Malvolio?"

Malvolio replied, "Sweet lady," and chuckled.

"Why are you smiling?" Olivia asked. "I sent for you on serious business."

This was true. She wanted to ask him how she should entertain Cesario.

"Serious, lady?" Malvolio said. "I could be serious. This cross-gartering does keep my blood from flowing freely in my legs, but if the cross-gartering pleases

62

the eyes of a certain person, then I say, as does the song, 'Please one, and please all.'"

The theme of the song was that all women want the same thing. The song may mean that all women want their own way — or that all women want something else.

"How are you, man?" Olivia asked. "What is the matter with you?"

"My mind is not black, but my legs are yellow," Malvolio replied.

He added, "It did come to his hands, and commands shall be executed."

This meant, *I did receive your letter, and I shall follow the instructions you wrote in it.*

He then said, "I think we do know the sweet Roman hand that is Italian calligraphy."

This meant, *Both of us know that the handwriting in the letter is your handwriting.*

Olivia asked, "Do you want to go to bed, Malvolio?"

"To bed?" Malvolio replied.

He sang, "*Yes, sweetheart, and I will come to you.*"

Olivia was shocked: "May God help you!"

Malvolio blew her some kisses.

Olivia said, "Why do you keep on smiling and kissing your hand?"

"How are you, Malvolio?" Maria asked.

Following the letter's instruments to cast off lower-class acquaintances, Malvolio said, "Do you think that I am going to speak to you? Do nightingales talk to crows?"

"Why are you talking so boldly to my lady, Olivia?" Maria asked.

Malvolio quoted the letter: "'*Be not afraid of greatness.*'"

He added, "That was well written."

Olivia asked, "What do you mean by that, Malvolio?"

"'*Some are born great,*'" he replied.

Olivia asked, "What?"

"'*Some achieve greatness.*'"

"What are you saying?"

"'*And some have greatness thrust upon them.*'"

"Heaven help you!"

"'*Remember who complimented your yellow stockings.*'"

"Your yellow stockings!" Olivia said.

"'*And wished to see thee cross-gartered.*'"

"Cross-gartered!"

"'*Do these things. Your fortune is made — if you want it to be made.*'"

"Did you say, 'Your fortune is mad'? Are you saying that I am mad?" Olivia asked.

"'*If you do not, do everything the way that you have always done them and make no change in your life. Go ahead and stay a steward.*'"

"You are suffering from midsummer madness."

One of Olivia's servants arrived and said, "Madam, I have brought back with me Duke Orsino's young messenger — with great difficulty. I could scarcely convince him to see you. He is now waiting for you."

"I will come to him right away," Olivia said.

She said to Maria, "This fellow needs to be looked after and cared for. Where is my uncle Toby? Have some of my servants take good care of Malvolio. I would not have anything bad happen to him for half of my dowry."

Olivia and Maria left, leaving Malvolio behind, alone in the garden.

Malvolio said to himself, "So, Olivia, do you understand me now? Do you know now that I will follow the instructions in your letter and be the kind of man you wrote that you wanted me to be?"

Malvolio believed that Olivia had pretended to be shocked at his behavior because Maria was present.

He added, "No less a man than a knight — Sir Toby — to look after me! This is part of Olivia's plan as recounted in the letter. She is sending Sir Toby to me so that I can be rude to him. She wrote about that in her letter: 'Your Fates have generously opened their hands; let your passion and courage embrace them. And, to accustom yourself to what you are likely to be, cast off your humble ways and appear fresh and new. Be disagreeable with a kinsman, be surly with servants; let your tongue speak about important matters; make yourself act eccentrically.' She also wrote down the manner of how I should look: a serious face, a dignified deportment, a slow manner of speech, dressing like a distinguished gentleman, and so forth. I have gotten her! But this is Jove's doing, and may Jove make me thankful! When she went away just now, she said, 'This fellow needs to be looked after and cared for.' She said 'fellow,' not Malvolio nor my job title, but 'fellow.' She is referring to me as an equal. Why, everything is coming together! Nothing — not even the tiniest thing or the tiniest part of a thing — can come between success and me! I have no obstacles and no impediments between success and me! I will marry Olivia! Well, Jove, not I, is the doer of this, and he is to be thanked."

Maria walked into the room, bringing with her Sir Toby and Fabian.

Sir Toby asked, "Where is he, in the name of sanctity?"

Sir Toby was going to pretend that Malvolio was possessed by demons, so now he pretended to fortify himself for the encounter by invoking sanctity.

He said, "If all the Devils of Hell be drawn together in a bunch, and Legion — the name of a group of Devils — himself has possessed Malvolio, yet I will speak to him."

"Here he is," Fabian said.

Sir Toby said to Malvolio, "How are you, sir? How are you, man?"

The letter had instructed Malvolio to cast off base acquaintances and to be rude to a kinsman — and if he married Olivia, Sir Toby would be his kinsman — and so he replied, "Go away, I don't want to speak with you. Let me enjoy my privacy. Go away."

Maria said, "Listen to how spookily the fiend possessing him speaks! Didn't I tell you that he is possessed? Sir Toby, my lady wants you to take care of him."

Malvolio said to himself, "Does she now?"

Sir Toby said to Maria and Fabian, "Quiet, please. We must deal gently with Malvolio."

He asked Malvolio, "How are you? How are you doing? Defy the Devil, who is inside you. Renounce him! Remember, the Devil is our enemy and an enemy to all Humankind."

"Do you even know what you are saying?" Malvolio replied.

Maria said to Sir Toby, "You spoke ill of the Devil — look at how badly Malvolio takes it! Pray to God that Malvolio is not bewitched!"

Fabian said, "Carry a sample of Malvolio's urine to the wise woman so she can analyze it."

"Good idea," Maria said, "and it shall be done tomorrow morning, I promise. My lady would not lose Malvolio for more than I can say."

"What are you saying!" Malvolio said.

"Oh, Lord!" Maria replied.

"Please, be quiet," Sir Toby said, "This is not the way to act in front of Malvolio. Can't you see that you are agitating him? Let me be alone with him."

"Treat him gently," Fabian said. "The fiend inside Malvolio is vicious and will not allow himself to be roughly treated."

Sir Toby said to Malvolio, "How are you, bawcock — my fine fellow! How are you doing, my chuck?"

"Sir!" Malvolio said, resentful about being talked down to and called silly and childish names.

"Biddy, come with me," Sir Toby said to Malvolio, "What, man! A dignified man ought not to play childish games with Satan. Satan is a dirty and dishonest coalman — hang him!"

"Get him to say his prayers, good Sir Toby," Maria said. "Get him to pray."

"You want me to say my prayers, hussy!" Malvolio said.

"No, Malvolio will not say his prayers," Maria said. "He is possessed by a Devil who cannot stand godliness."

"Go and hang yourselves, all of you!" Malvolio said. "You are idle and shallow things: I am not of your element — I am superior to you! You shall learn more later."

He left.

Sir Toby said, "Is it really true that our trick is working so well?"

Fabian said, "If this were played upon a stage right now, I would condemn it as an improbable fiction."

Sir Toby said, "He completely and totally believes that Olivia wrote the letter!"

Maria said, "Let us quickly continue the trick. Soon our joke will become known, and it will be spoiled."

"Should we do that?" Fabian asked. "What if he really and truly becomes insane?"

Maria said, "The house will be quieter."

She meant that she would no longer have to listen to Malvolio's criticisms of her. The house would likely become noisier with no one to at least attempt to restrain Sir Toby's late-night parties. Also, if Malvolio were to become insane, he would likely be locked up in a dark room, where he would howl. The dark room would be in a place where few people, if any, could hear him.

Sir Toby said, "Come on. We will have Malvolio tied up and placed in a dark room — the standard treatment for treating insanity. Olivia already believes that Malvolio is insane, and so we can continue to treat Malvolio however we like until we get tired of this joke and show mercy to him. When we get tired of laughing at him, we will let our trick become known by all and crown you, Maria, as a finder of madmen."

He saw Sir Andrew coming toward him and said, "Look who's coming."

"Here is more merriment," Fabian said.

Sir Andrew came to them with his letter in his hand and said, "Here is the challenge — read it. I promise that vinegar and pepper are in it."

"Is it so saucy?" Fabian joked. "Saucy" means both spiced like a sauce and insulting.

Sir Andrew, who failed to get the joke, said, "Yes, it is, I promise you that. Read it."

Sir Toby said, "Give it to me."

He read out loud, "*Youth, whatever else you are, you are a scurvy fellow.*"

Fabian commented, "That is good, and valiant. It shows courage and determination." He would praise the letter no matter how silly it got.

Sir Toby continued reading out loud, "*Don't wonder at or be surprised by what I call you. I will not tell you why I call you that.*"

"This is a good note," Fabian said. "It keeps you on the right side of the law. You will not be sued."

Sir Toby continued reading out loud, "*You have talked with the lady Olivia. I have seen that she treats you nicely. But you lie in your throat — that is not why I am writing you and challenging you to fight me.*"

If Cesario were lying in his throat when he talked to Olivia, he would be lying when he said that he did not love her.

Fabian said, "Very brief, and very good sense." To Sir Toby, he whispered, "Sense — less."

Sir Toby continued reading out loud, "*I will ambush you when you go home. If it should happen that you kill me —*"

"Good," Fabian said.

Sir Andrew thought that Fabian meant that the half-sentence was well written, but Fabian was joking that it would be a good thing if Sir Andrew were killed.

Sir Toby continued reading out loud, "*If it should happen that you kill me, you kill me like a rogue and a villain.*"

Fabian enjoyed the sentence. The phrase "a rogue and a villain" was ambiguous. It could refer to Cesario — or to Sir Andrew.

Fabian said, "You are still keeping yourself on the right side of the law. Good work."

Sir Toby continued reading out loud, "*Fare thee well; and God have mercy upon one of our souls! He may have mercy upon mine, but my hope is better.*"

Fabian thought, *Funny! Sir Andrew thought that he was writing that he hopes to survive, but instead he wrote that he hopes to be damned to Hell.*

Sir Toby continued reading out loud, "*Look to yourself. I am your friend, to the extent that you treat me as a friend.*"

Fabian thought, *Sir Andrew is trying to say that the quarrel is all Cesario's fault.*

Sir Toby continued reading out loud, "*Signed, Your sworn enemy, ANDREW AGUECHEEK.*"

Sir Toby said, "If this letter does not move Cesario, his legs must be paralyzed. I will give him your letter."

"You will soon have a good opportunity to do that," Maria said. "Cesario is talking to Olivia, and he will soon leave her."

"Go, Sir Andrew," Sir Toby said, "Keep watch for Cesario in the corner of the garden. Act like a sheriff's official who arrests debtors. Don't let him get away. As soon as you see him, draw your sword, and as you draw your sword, swear horribly. It often happens that a terrible oath, when pronounced boldly, gives a man a better reputation for courage than he would have gotten if he had actually fought. Go now."

Sir Andrew said, "I'm really good at swearing," and left.

Sir Toby said, "I will not give Cesario Sir Andrew's letter. Cesario's behavior shows that he is a young gentleman of intelligence and education. His employment as a go-between for Orsino and Olivia confirms that. Therefore, if Cesario were to read this letter, which is so silly, it would not terrify him because he would realize that its writer is an idiot. Instead, sir, I will deliver Sir Andrew's challenge in person, orally. I will say that Sir Andrew is famous for his courage, and I will make Cesario believe — he is young, so he will believe whatever I tell him — that Sir Andrew is known for his rage, skill, fury, and impetuosity. Both Cesario and Sir Andrew will be so frightened of each other that a mere look from them will kill the other, just as the mythological creatures known as basilisks are said to be able to kill with a look."

Olivia and Viola now entered the garden.

Fabian said, "Here come Cesario and your niece. Wait until he leaves, and then go after him."

"In the meantime, I will think about what to say to Cesario," Sir Toby said. "I will make up some horrible challenge for him."

Sir Toby, Fabian, and Maria all left the garden, leaving Viola and Olivia alone. Sir Andrew watched the two from a distance.

Olivia said to Viola, "I have said too much to you and to your heart of stone, and I have unwisely risked my reputation. I may have done the wrong thing, but my fault is so headstrong and powerful that it mocks reproof. I may have done the wrong thing in telling you that I love you, but I can't regret it."

"Your passion for me compels you to tell me that you love me," Viola said. "Orsino's passion for you compels him to send you the message that he loves you."

Olivia said, "Here, wear this jeweled miniature for me — it is my picture. Don't refuse it. It has no tongue to vex you. I ask that you come to me again tomorrow. You can ask nothing of me that I will deny you except that which honor requires me to deny you."

Viola did not take the locket. She said, "I ask you for nothing but this — that you love Orsino."

"How can I honorably give him that which I have already given to you?"

"I will return that gift to you."

Olivia said, "Well, come again tomorrow. Fare thee well. A fiend like you might bear my soul to Hell."

She went back inside her house.

Sir Toby and Fabian had been watching. Now they approached Viola.

"May God save you," Sir Toby said.

"And you, sir," Viola replied.

Sir Toby said to Viola, "Whatever skill you have in fencing, now is the time for you to use it. I don't know what wrongs you have done to him, but I know that he is full of hatred for you and that he is as bloodthirsty as a dog hunting its prey. He is waiting for you there in the corner of the garden. Unsheathe your rapier and quickly prepare to defend yourself because your enemy is quick, skillful, and deadly."

"You must be mistaken, sir," Viola replied. "I am sure that no man has any reason to quarrel with me. I can remember no offense that I have committed against any man."

Sir Toby replied, "Your enemy thinks otherwise, I assure you; therefore, if you value your life, be on guard because your enemy has youth, strength, skill, and anger."

"Please, sir, who is he?"

"He is a knight," Sir Toby said. "He became a knight not through his service in battle, but through domestic service. Nevertheless, he is a Devil when it comes to his private quarrels. He has killed three men and sent their souls to either Heaven or Hell. Right now, his anger at you is so implacable that it can be satisfied only by pangs of death and entombment in a burial vault. His motto is 'Kill, or be killed.'"

"I will go into the house and ask Olivia for someone to escort and protect me," Viola said. "I am no fighter. I have heard that some men start quarrels without cause on purpose as a test of their own and other men's courage. This man must be like that."

"Sir, no, he is not," Sir Toby said. "His anger comes from a very notable insult, and therefore you must fight him. I will not allow you to go back inside the house unless you first fight me, and so you might as well fight him. Therefore, either draw your sword and fight him, or admit to your cowardice and never again wear a sword."

"This is both rude and unintelligible," Viola said. "I ask you to do me a favor: Find out from the knight what he thinks is my offense to him. Whatever it is, it is accidental and was not done on purpose."

"I will do so," Sir Toby said, "Mr. Fabian, stay by Cesario until my return."

Sir Toby wanted Fabian to keep Cesario from either going into Olivia's house or running away.

Sir Toby left to talk to Sir Andrew.

Viola said to Fabian, "Please, sir, do you know anything about this?"

"I know that the knight is angry at you — so angry that he wants to kill you — but I do not know the reason why."

"What kind of man is he?"

"If you look at him, you would not think that he is a courageous fighter, but you will change your mind as soon as you see him in action. He is, indeed, sir, the most skillful, bloody, and deadly enemy that you could possibly have found in any part of Illyria. Will you walk with me to him and meet with him? I will make your peace with him if I can."

"I would appreciate it if you can make peace," Viola said. "I am the kind of person who would rather meet Sir Priest than Sir Knight. I don't care what that makes people think about my courage."

Meanwhile, Sir Toby was talking to Sir Andrew.

Sir Toby said, "Why, man, Cesario is a very Devil; I have not seen such a virago — he may look feminine, but he fights like a seasoned male warrior. I had a practice bout with him, and he thrust his sword at me with such a deadly motion, that I could not defend against it. When I thrust back at him, he thrust again and would have killed me a second time if our fight had been for real. He stabs you with his sword just as surely as your feet hit the ground they step on. They say that he has been fencer to the Shah of Persia."

"Damn, I'll not fight him," Sir Andrew said.

Sir Toby said, "That's a wise decision, but now Cesario is so angry that he will not be pacified. Look! Fabian can scarcely hold him yonder — Cesario is eager to kill you."

Fabian was holding Viola's arm as she struggled to escape and run away.

"If I had known he was so brave and so skillful in fencing, I would have seen him damned before I would have challenged him. If he will forget about it, I'll give him my horse: Grey Capilet."

"I'll see what I can do," Sir Toby said. "Stand here, and put on a show of bravery. I intend that this shall end without the loss of life."

He walked toward Fabian and Viola, who were now walking toward him, and he thought, *I will end up riding Sir Andrew's horse as well as riding Sir Andrew.*

Sir Toby said quietly to Fabian, "I can get Sir Andrew's horse — he wants me to settle this quarrel. I have persuaded him that Cesario is a Devil when it comes to a fight."

Fabian said quietly to Sir Toby, "Cesario is just as scared of Sir Andrew as Sir Andrew is of him. Cesario hyperventilates and looks pale, as if a bear were chasing him."

Sir Toby said quietly to Viola, "There's no remedy, sir. I can do nothing to stop this fight. He has thought about the reason for this quarrel, and he finds that it is now scarcely worth talking of, but he will fight you because he made an oath to fight you. Therefore, draw your sword, but be aware that he is fighting you only because of his oath, and he promises that he will not hurt you."

Viola thought, *May God defend me! I am almost ready to tell them what part I lack of a man.*

Fabian advised Viola, "Give ground and retreat if you see him really furious."

Sir Toby said quietly, "Come, Sir Andrew, you can't get out of this. The gentleman will, for his honor's sake, have one bout with you. By the rules of dueling, he cannot avoid fighting you, but as he is a gentleman and a soldier, he has promised me that he will not hurt you. Come on. It's time to fight him."

Sir Andrew said, "Pray God he keep his oath!"

Viola said, "It is against my will."

Sir Andrew thought that Cesario meant that it was against his will that he keep his oath not to hurt Sir Andrew, but Viola meant that it was against her will that she was fighting at all.

Sir Andrew and Viola drew their swords. Antonio, who was looking for Sebastian, saw them from the street. Thinking that Viola was her brother, Sebastian, he entered Olivia's garden and said to Sir Andrew, "Put up your sword. If this young gentleman has done any offence, I take the fault on me. If you have offended him, then I defy you for him."

Sir Toby asked, "You, sir, who are you?"

Antonio replied, "I am one, sir, who for his deep friendship for this man will do more than you have heard me say to you that I will do."

Angry that his fun had been interrupted, Sir Toby said, "If you are willing to fight in his place, I am willing to fight in Sir Andrew's place."

Sir Toby and Antonio drew their swords, but Fabian said to Sir Toby, "Wait! Here come two officers of the law!"

Sir Toby said to Antonio, "I won't fight you right now, but I will after the officers leave."

Viola said to Sir Andrew, "Please, sir, put your sword back is its scabbard, if you please."

He replied, "Indeed, I will, sir, and, as for that which I promised you, I will be as good as my word: My horse will bear you easily and reins well."

Viola was mystified by the comment, but everyone put their swords back in their scabbards.

The first officer pointed to Antonio and said, "This is the man; do your duty."

The second officer said, "Antonio, I arrest you in the name of Duke Orsino."

"You have mistaken me for someone else," Antonio said.

The first officer replied, "No, not at all. I know your face well, though now you have no sea cap on your head. Take him away: He knows that I know who he is."

Antonio said to the officers, "I will go quietly."

Antonio said to Viola, "This is a result of my seeking you, but that is the way it is. I will face the consequences. I will either defend myself well or pay the penalty. However, I worry about you. What will you do now that my circumstances force me to ask you to return my money? I grieve much more about not being to help you than I grieve for myself."

Viola looked shocked at these words. She had never seen Antonio before.

Antonio said to her, "You seem shocked, but don't worry about me."

The second officer said, "Come on, sir. Let's go."

Antonio said to Viola, "I must ask you for some of that money."

Viola replied, "What money, sir? For the kindness you have given to me here, when you offered to fight this man for me, and in part because I pity you in your present trouble, I'll lend you some of the little money I have. I don't have much money, but I'll divide it with you. Here, take half of the money I have."

The amount of money was much less that what Antonio had given to Sebastian.

Antonio said to Viola, "Are you going to pretend not to know me? Is it possible that you will do that despite all that I have done for you? I have been arrested, and you ought to help me. Don't make me demean myself by reminding you of all the things that I have done to help you."

"Other than the good deed you have done for me just now, I know of nothing that you have done to help me," Viola said. "I do not know your voice or your face. I hate ingratitude more in a man than lying, vanity, babbling drunkenness, or any other vice that our weak human nature is susceptible to."

"Oh, my God!" Antonio said.

The second officer said, "Come, sir, let's go."

"Let me say a few words," Antonio said. "This youth whom you see here I snatched out of the jaws of death. He was half dead, but I lovingly nursed him back to health, and devoted myself to him because he looked so noble and good."

The first officer replied, "What is that to us? The time is passing. We need to leave!"

Antonio said, "But this man who seemed to be a god turns out to be a vile idol. You shame your good looks, Sebastian. The only real blemish is a blemish of the mind. The only real deformity is an unnatural hardness of heart:

"In nature there's no blemish but the mind;

"None can be called deformed but the unkind.

"Virtue and beauty are supposed to be synonymous, but some evil people are beautiful; they are like empty trunks whose exterior is decorated by the Devil:

"Virtue is beauty, but the beauteous evil

"Are empty trunks overflourished by the Devil."

The first officer said, "Antonio is becoming insane. Let's take him away! Come with us, Antonio."

"Take me away," Antonio said.

He left with the two officers of the law.

Viola said to herself, "He speaks with such passion that I think that he believes what he says. But I don't."

But then an explanation for Antonio's words occurred to her: "I hope that it may be true. My brother, Sebastian, may still be alive, and Antonio may have thought that I am he."

Sir Toby had been amused by Antonio's couplets. He said, "Come with me, Sir Andrew and Fabian. We will say among ourselves a couplet or two of most sage saws."

Viola said to herself, "Antonio said the name Sebastian. Whenever I look into a mirror, I see the image of my brother. We look almost exactly alike. We have the same features, the same face. We are dressed in the same style and color of clothing and with the same ornaments because I imitated him when I disguised myself as a man. If my brother is still alive, then tempests are kind and waves are fresh and filled with love. Unkind tempests and salt waves have foregone their ordinary attributes, if my brother is alive."

Viola exited.

Sir Toby said, "Cesario is a very dishonest and paltry boy, and he is more cowardly than is a hare. Cesario shows that he is dishonorable because he is doing nothing to help his friend in need and even denies knowing him. As for Cesario's cowardice, ask Fabian about it."

"It is true," Fabian said. "Cesario is a coward, a most devout coward. He is as devoted to cowardice as if it were his religion."

Happy to hear that Cesario is a coward, Sir Andrew said, "By God, I'll go after him and beat him."

Sir Toby said, "Do that, Sir Andrew, fight him. Beat him soundly. But do not draw your sword against him."

"I swear that I will —"

Sir Andrew left.

Fabian said to Sir Toby, "Come on. Let's go and watch."

"I bet you that nothing will come of it. Those two still will not fight."

They followed Sir Andrew.

CHAPTER 4

— 4.1 —

Sebastian and Feste were arguing in front of Olivia's house. Olivia had sent Feste to find Cesario and bring him back to her, and Feste thought that Sebastian was Cesario.

Feste said, "Are you trying to make me believe that I was not sent for you?"

Sebastian replied, "Go away. You are a foolish fellow. Stay out of my way."

"You are certainly stubborn about denying who you are! No, I do not know who you are. No, my lady did not send me to get you. No, your name is not Cesario. No, my nose is not my nose. According to you, nothing that is so is so."

"Please, go and vent your folly somewhere else. You do not know me."

"Vent my folly! You have heard those words from some important and learned man and now you are applying them to a fool. Vent my folly! I am afraid that affectation and foppery will spread all over the world. Please, stop denying that you know me — we have met and talked before. Tell me what I shall vent to my lady, Olivia. Shall I vent to her that you are coming and will see her?"

"Please, foolish fellow, depart from me. Here is a coin for you. If you keep bothering me, I will give you worse payment."

"Truly, you have a generous hand," Feste said, remembering the two coins that Viola had given to him earlier. "These wise men who give fools money get for themselves a good reputation — if they keep on giving money for fourteen years."

Sir Andrew, Sir Toby, and Fabian now came running up to Sebastian. Like Feste, they thought that Sebastian was Cesario.

Sir Andrew said to Sebastian, "Now, sir, I have met you again."

He hit Sebastian and said, "That's for you."

Sebastian drew his dagger and hit an astonished Sir Andrew three times with the hilt, saying, "That's for you! And that! And that!"

He then said, "Are all the people in Illyria insane?"

Sir Toby did not want Sebastian to keep hitting his source of income. He said, "Stop, sir, or I'll throw your dagger over the house."

Things were starting to get serious, and Feste said, "I am going to tell Olivia all about this. I would not be in some of your shoes for two pennies."

Feste was loyal to Olivia and knew that she would want to know about fights on her property.

Sir Toby had grabbed hold of Sebastian. Sir Toby said, "Stop your fighting."

Sir Andrew said, "Let him go. I can fight him another way. I'll have an action of battery brought against him, if there is any law in Illyria. I struck him first, but that doesn't matter."

"Let go of me," Sebastian said to Sir Toby.

"I will not let you go. Come, my young warrior, put up your dagger. You are too eager to fight."

"I will be free from you," Sebastian said.

He struggled, got himself free of Sir Toby's grip, drew his sword, and said, "What will you do now? If you dare to keep on bothering me, draw your sword."

"What!" Sir Toby said. "In that case, I must have an ounce or two of your impudent blood from you."

Alerted by Feste, Olivia came running.

She said, "Sir Toby, stop! On your life, I order you to stop."

Sir Toby stopped. Olivia gave him free room and board. He did not want to push her too far. He was her uncle, but she held the power and owned the property.

"Madam!" he said.

"Will it always be this way?" Olivia asked. "Ungracious wretch, you are fit only for the mountains and the barbarous caves, where good manners and etiquette are never learned or practiced. Get out of my sight!"

Olivia said to Sebastian, "Don't be offended, dear Cesario."

Noticing that Sir Toby was still present, she yelled at him, "Rudesby, lout, be gone!"

Sir Toby, Sir Andrew, and Fabian all left.

Olivia said to Sebastian, "Please, good friend, let yourself be guided by your calm wisdom and not by your anger at this uncivil and unjust attack against you. Come with me into my house, and I will tell you of many stupid and demeaning pranks that this ruffian has clumsily dreamed up. When you hear about them, you will probably smile at this one, too."

Sebastian was hesitant about going with a strange woman, but Olivia said, "I will not allow you to do anything but go with me. Do not deny me my wish."

Olivia believed that she was talking to Cesario. She also believed that her heart was not her own — she was in love with and had given her heart to Cesario.

She said to Sebastian, "Curse that ruffian. He made my heart jump like a hart that has been startled and driven out into the open by hunters."

Sebastian thought, *How sweet and beautiful this woman is! But what is going on? Either I am mad, or else this is a dream. If it is a dream, then let me drink from the Lethe River of mythology so that I will forget what reality is and remain with this sweet and beautiful woman in my dream.*

Olivia said to him, "Please, come with me. I wish that you would allow me to guide you."

Sebastian said, "Madam, I will."

Happy, Olivia said, "You have said it! Now live it!"

Malvolio had been locked in a small, dark room in Olivia's house. In a room adjoining that room, Maria and Feste were talking. Maria was carrying a false beard and clerical clothing.

Maria said to Feste, "Please, put on this gown and this beard. I want to make Malvolio believe that you are Sir Topas, the curate. Put on these things quickly. I will go and get Sir Toby so that he can enjoy the fun."

Feste said, "Well, I will put these things on, and I will disguise myself in them. A disguise is a kind of dissembling, and I wish that I were the first person who ever dissembled in such a gown. Too many clerics have been corrupt."

He was in an odd position. A professional fool is a kind of servant and must keep the people around him happy. He needed to be loyal to Olivia, who was the most important person in the house, but he also needed to humor Sir Toby, who was a source of income. As for Malvolio, he had tried to get Olivia to fire Feste, and Feste would like to have revenge.

Feste put on the fake beard and the cleric's gown and said, "I am not distinguished enough to play the role well, nor lean enough to be thought a good student; still, to be said to be an honest man and a good host is almost as good as being said to be a dutiful man and a great scholar. I hear the co-conspirators coming."

Sir Toby and Maria entered the room.

Sir Toby said to Feste, "May Jove bless you, Master Parson."

"*Bonos dies*, Sir Toby," Feste said in deliberately bad Latin, thinking that a real parson ought to know Latin well.

Feste then began to mock philosophical language: "As the old hermit of Prague, who never saw pen and ink, very wittily said to a niece of King Gorboduc, 'That that is, is.' I, being Master Parson, am Master Parson. After all, what is 'that' but 'that' and what is 'is' but 'is'?"

"Malvolio is your prey," Sir Toby said. "Go after him."

Disguising his voice, Feste called, "Hello! May there be peace in this prison!"

Sir Toby said to Maria, "The knave counterfeits well; he is a good knave."

Hearing Feste's voice, Malvolio, locked but not bound in the dark room, yelled, "Who calls there?"

Feste said, "I am Sir Topas the curate, and I have come to visit Malvolio the lunatic."

"Sir Topas, Sir Topas, good Sir Topas, go to my lady, Olivia, and take her a message from me."

Feste pretended that Malvolio was possessed and that the Devil within Malvolio was speaking. Feste yelled, "Out, hyperbolical fiend! See how you are vexing this man! Fiend, can you talk about nothing but women?"

Sir Toby complimented Feste, "Well said, Master Parson."

Malvolio said, "Sir Topas, never was a man so much wronged as I am. Good Sir Topas, do not think that I am mad. They say that I am insane, and they have laid me here in hideous darkness."

"Satan, you are dishonest," Feste said. "I call you dishonest instead of the stronger word 'liar' because I am one of those gentle ones who will treat the Devil himself with courtesy. Did you say that this place is dark?"

"As dark as Hell itself, Sir Topas," Malvolio said.

"Why, it has bay windows that are as transparent as solid barricades, and the upper windows facing toward the south-north are as white and transparent as ebony wood, so why are you complaining of darkness?"

"Sir Topas, I am not mad. I say again to you: This place is dark."

"Madman, you are wrong. I say that there is no darkness except for ignorance and you are more ignorant than were the Egyptians in the fog that caused three days of darkness."

Malvolio replied, "I say that this place is as dark as ignorance, even though ignorance were as dark as Hell; and I say, there was never any man more abused than I am. I am no more mad than you are. Test me and see if I am mad. Ask me a question."

Feste asked, "What is the opinion of the ancient Greek philosopher Pythagoras concerning wild fowl?"

"He believed in reincarnation and that the soul of our grandmother might perhaps be in a bird."

"What do you think of his theory?"

"I think nobly of the soul, and in no way approve of his theory."

"Fare thee well," Feste said. "Remain you always in darkness. You shall believe in the theory of Pythagoras before I will believe that you are sane, and you will be afraid to kill a really stupid woodcock, lest you dispossess the soul of your grandmother. Fare thee well."

"Sir Topas! Sir Topas!" Malvolio called as Feste seemed to walk away.

Actually, Feste walked only a few steps away, just enough to be out of Malvolio's hearing if Feste and others spoke quietly.

Sir Toby complimented Feste, "My most exquisite Sir Topas! You performed your role perfectly well!"

Feste said, "I can sail any sea. I can perform all roles."

Maria said, "You could have performed the role without wearing the false beard and the parson's gown. Malvolio cannot see you."

The false beard and the gown had been Maria's idea. Now she was mocking Feste for doing what she had told him to do.

Sir Toby said to Feste, "Talk to Malvolio in your own voice, and bring me word about what happens."

He added, "I wish that this joke was over and that we were well rid of this knavery. If we could release Malvolio from this prison without too much trouble, I would do so. I am now in so much trouble with Olivia, my niece, that I cannot much longer continue this joke, although I would like to."

He said to Maria, "Come by and by to my chamber."

Sir Toby and Maria departed, leaving Feste alone with Malvolio.

Feste had his orders, and he followed them.

In his own voice, he sang about a woman who first loved one man and then loved another:

"*Hey, Robin, jolly Robin,*

"*Tell me how your lady does.*"

Malvolio recognized Feste's voice and called, "Fool!"

Feste sang, "*My lady is unkind, certainly.*"

Malvolio called, "Fool!"

"*Alas, why is she so?*"

"Fool, I say!"

"*She loves another.*"

Feste's song was about the inconstancy of some loves. A person can love one person for a while, and then end up loving another person.

Feste stopped singing and asked, "Who is calling me?"

Malvolio said, "Good fool, if you would like to do something for me that will be well rewarded, get me some candles, and a pen, ink, and paper. As I am a gentleman, I will reward you for it."

"Are you Master Malvolio?"

"Yes, good fool."

"Sir, how did you fall out of your five wits: common wit, imagination, fantasy, estimation, and memory?"

"Fool, never was a man so notoriously and obviously abused: I am as well in my wits, fool, as you are."

"Only as well in your wits as I am?" Feste said. "Then you must be mad indeed, if you are no better in your wits than a fool."

"They are treating me like a thing, not like a person," Malvolio said. "They keep me in darkness, they send ministers to me, and they do everything they can to drive me out of my mind. They are asses!"

"Be careful what you say," Feste said. "Sir Topas is here."

Using the voice of Sir Topas, Feste said, "Malvolio, Malvolio, may Heaven restore your wits! Try to go to sleep, and stop talking your bibble babble."

Malvolio called, "Sir Topas!"

Feste pretended to be Sir Topas, who he pretended was talking to Feste, "Don't talk to him, good fellow."

In his own voice, Feste said, "Who, I, sir? Not I, sir. God be with you, good Sir Topas."

In the voice of Sir Topas, Feste said, "Be well."

In his own voice, Feste said, "I will, sir, I will."

"Fool, fool, fool, I say!" Malvolio called, afraid that Feste was leaving.

"Sir, be quiet," Feste said. "What do you want to say, sir? Sir Topaz has just rebuked me for talking to you."

"Good fool, get me some candles and a pen, ink, and paper. I tell you that I am as well in my wits as any man in Illyria."

"I wish that that were true, sir."

"I swear that I am sane," Malvolio said. "Good fool, get me a pen, ink, paper, and candles. Deliver to Olivia the letter that I will write. I will reward you more than you have ever been rewarded for the delivery of a letter."

"I will help you," Feste said. "I will get you what you need. But tell me the truth: Are you really mad? Or are you just pretending to be insane?"

"Believe me, I am not insane. I am telling you the truth."

"I don't believe you. I will never believe a madman until I see his brains. For one thing, I want to verify whether or not he has brains. Nevertheless, I will fetch you candles and a pen and paper and ink."

"I will pay you well," Malvolio said. "Please, go and get me what I need."

Feste left Malvolio. Throughout their encounter, Malvolio had been angry, but dignified and controlled.

Sir Toby and Maria were pretending that Malvolio was possessed by the Devil. If this were true, Malvolio would need an exorcism to cast the Devil out of his body. As he left Malvolio, Feste sang a song about old Vice, the son of the Devil, driving the Devil away with a wooden dagger:

"I am gone, sir,

"And quickly, sir,

"I'll be with you again,

"In a trice,

"Like to the old Vice,

"In order to help you resist the Devil;

"Who, with dagger of lath,

"In his rage and his wrath,

"Cries, 'Ah, ha!' to the Devil:

"Like a mad lad,

"'Pare your fingernails, Dad;

"'Adieu, good man Devil.'"

Alone in Olivia's garden, Sebastian marveled at his good fortune. He was a stranger in a strange land, but a sweet and beautiful lady who was a rich Countess had taken him in — and she appeared to have fallen in love with him at first sight. He wondered whether this were real.

He said to himself, "This is the air; that is the glorious Sun; this is the pearl she gave me — I feel it and I see it. I am enveloped in wonder, but I am not enveloped in madness.

"I wonder where Antonio is. I could not find him at the Elephant Inn, yet he had been there; and there I learned that he had left to walk the streets and find me. If he were here, he could give me golden advice. His counsel now might do me golden service. My mind agrees with my senses. Somehow there has been a mistake somewhere, but I am not mad. This unexpected and sudden flood of good luck exceeds all precedent and likelihood and so I am ready not to believe my own eyes and I am ready to distrust my reason when it tells me that I am not mad and that this lady is not mad. However, if this lady were insane, she could not run her house, command her servants, and handle her household affairs and make decisions with such a smooth, discreet, and stable bearing as I see she does. Something here is deceptive, and I don't know what it is. But here comes the lady now."

Olivia and a priest walked up to Sebastian.

Olivia said to Sebastian, "Forgive me for my haste, but if your intentions toward me are consistent with marriage, go with me and this holy man now into the chapel. There, before the priest and underneath the chapel's consecrated roof, marry me and promise to be true to me so that my most jealous and too doubtful soul may be at peace. The priest shall conceal our marriage until you are willing that it be made public. At that time, we will have a public wedding that is suitable for a Countess. What do you say? Are you willing to marry me?"

"I will follow this good man, and I will go with you. I will marry you, and I will always be true and faithful to you."

Olivia said to the priest, "Lead the way, good father; and may the Sun shine and Heaven bless this marriage."

CHAPTER 5

— 5.1 —

In front of Olivia's house, Feste and Fabian were talking.

Fabian said to Feste, "Please let me see Malvolio's letter."

"Fabian, grant me a request first."

"Anything you want."

"Do not desire to see this letter."

"It's as if you gave me a dog and then as recompense asked for the dog back again."

Duke Orsino, Viola, Curio, and others arrived. Finally, Orsino was going to see Olivia face to face and do his own courting.

Orsino asked, "Are you servants of the Lady Olivia?"

Feste replied, "Yes, we decorate her household."

Recognizing Feste, Orsino said, "I know you well. How are you, my good fellow?"

"Sir, I am better off because of my enemies and worse off because of my friends."

"Don't you mean the contrary?" Orsino asked. "Aren't we better off because of our friends?"

"No, sir, we are worse off."

"How can that be?"

"Friends praise me and make an ass of me, but my enemies tell me plainly I am an ass. When I associate with my enemies, I profit by knowing myself better. When I associate with my friends, I am abused and made to do foolish things."

Feste thought, *This is true. Sir Toby and Maria, who are supposed to be friends of mine, made me do something bad to Malvolio, although I admit I did not resist. Cesario, however, is not supposed to be my friend because he serves Orsino, who bothers Olivia, whom I serve. But I profited by speaking to Cesario; we shared our jests and wisdom — and he tipped me well.*

Feste added, "If four negatives make two positives, I am worse off because of my friends and better off because of my enemies. Four negatives are a good thing. If I ask to kiss a woman, and she says, 'no, no,' the rules of grammar and of logic conclude that she is saying one yes. If I receive four noes, then logically I get two kisses. And when two quarreling lovers quarrel and then make up, they kiss. Their four lips that have been saying 'no' now become two mouths that kiss and say 'yes.'"

"This is excellent foolery," Orsino said.

"Indeed, it is not. You seem to be one of my friends."

"I do not want to be a friend who makes you worse off," Orsino said. "Here is gold for you."

He gave Feste a coin.

"Except that it would be double-dealing, sir, I wish that you would make it another," Feste said.

"To be 'double-dealing' — duplicitous — would be bad counsel," Orsino said. "And so would be, financially speaking, paying twice for something."

"Realize that your grace is in your pocket, sir," Feste said. "Feel free to go ahead and fish it out."

"Well, I will be so much a sinner as to be a double-dealer," Orsino said. He reached into his pocket, took out a coin, and gave it to Feste, saying, "Here is the second coin that I have dealt to you."

Feste counted one through three in Latin, "*Primo, secundo, tertio*. These words make a good beginning. Third time lucky, and the third pays for all. In music, triple time is good to dance to, and the bells of Saint Benedict's Church, sir, may put you in mind to be generous: They toll one, two, three."

"You can fool no more money out of me in this particular game," Orsino said, smiling, "but if you will let Olivia know that I am here to speak with her, and if you bring her to me, it may further awaken my generosity."

"Sir, let your generosity sleep until I return again. I am going, sir, to get Olivia for you, but I would not have you think that my desire for coins is the sin of covetousness."

Feste thought, *Getting a really good tip is an art. Getting any tip is a necessity.*

He added, "As you say, sir, let your generosity take a nap for now, but don't worry, I will awaken it soon."

Feste left.

Viola said to Orsino, "Here comes the man, sir, who rescued me when Sir Andrew wanted to duel me."

Some officers of the law brought Antonio to Orsino.

Orsino said, "That face of his I do remember well, but when I saw it last, it was in the smoke of war besmeared as black as the face of Vulcan, the blacksmith god. He was the captain of a little boat with shallow draught and of little worth, but with that boat he grappled with and did such damage to the most noble ship of our fleet that we his enemies envied his bravery and despite our losses proclaimed his honor and gave him a great reputation for valor. Why is he here?"

The first officer said, "Orsino, this is that Antonio who captured the *Phoenix* and her freight from Candia, the capital of Crete. He also boarded the *Tiger*, in which encounter your young nephew Titus lost his leg. Here in our streets, he recklessly disregarded his notoriety in our country and the shame that comes from dueling in a private brawl, and so we arrested him."

Viola said to Orsino, "He did me kindness, sir. He drew his sword so he could fight for me, but afterward, he spoke strange things to me. I don't know the reason except that he must be mad."

Orsino said to Antonio, "Notable pirate! You salt-water thief! What foolish boldness brought you here to us, whom you, with bloody and harmful actions that have been costly to us, have made your enemies? Why have you put yourself into our hands and made yourself subject to our mercy?"

"Orsino, noble sir, allow me to shake off these names you give me. I, Antonio, have never been a thief or a pirate, though I confess that I have been, for good reason, your enemy. A kind of witchcraft drew me to Illyria. That most ungrateful boy there by your side, from the rough sea's enraged and foamy mouth I did save."

He looked at Viola and then added, "He was close to death and seemed to be past hope. I saved his life and I gave him all my friendship without reservation. I dedicated myself to him. Because of my devoted friendship, in order to serve him I came here and exposed myself to the danger of this hostile town. I drew my sword to defend him when thugs beset him. After I was arrested, he did not want to face any danger and so his ungrateful cunning made him deny that he ever knew me. In the time that it takes to blink, he pretended to be a stranger who had not seen me for the last twenty years. In addition, he refused to give me my own money, which I had given him to hold and to use not half an hour previously."

"How could these things even be possible?" Viola said.

"When did this young man first come to my town?" Orsino asked.

"He came here today, sir," Antonio said. "During the three months previous to today, he and I have always been together, day and night, with not even a minute of separation between us."

Olivia and her attendants now walked toward Orsino and the others.

Orsino said, "Here comes the Countess. Heaven now walks on earth."

He said to Antonio, "As for you, your words are insane. For the past three months, this youth has been my servant. We will talk more about this later."

He said to the officers of the law, "Take Antonio to one side. I will now talk with Olivia."

Olivia said to Orsino, "How can I help you, sir? Don't ask for what I can't give you — my love — but otherwise I will gladly help you."

She said to Viola, whom she thought was Sebastian, whom she had married, "You should be here by my side."

Shocked, Viola said, "Madam!"

Orsino began speaking, "Gracious Olivia —"

But Olivia interrupted him and said to Viola, "What do you say, Cesario?"

Orsino wanted to speak to Olivia, but she said, "Not now," and then she looked at Viola.

Viola said, "My lord — Orsino — wants to speak to you; my duty is to be quiet while he speaks."

Olivia said to Orsino, "If you are here to sing the same old words to the same old tune, the experience will be as burdensome and distasteful to my ears as would be howling after I have heard beautiful music."

"Are you still so cruel, Olivia?"

"I am still so constant."

"Constant to what?" Orsino said. "Perverseness? You are perverse in constantly refusing my love for you. You, lady, are cruel. My soul has made more sacrifices on your ungrateful and unpropitious altars than a lover has ever made before. What shall I do?"

"Do whatever you want, as long as it is suitable for you," Olivia said.

"Why shouldn't I, if I had the heart to do it, act like the Egyptian thief who, when he was close to death, decided to kill the woman he loved?" Orsino said. "That kind of savage jealousy can sometimes seem to be noble. But listen to me now. Since you reject my love, and since I know from your words at least in part why you keep rejecting my love, I am going to take away from you that young man who has taken the place in your heart that ought to be mine. Go ahead and keep your cold heart of marble. But this young man, this Cesario, I will keep away from you. You will never see him again. I care deeply for this young man, but I am angry because he has taken your love — love that ought to be mine."

Orsino then said to Cesario, "Come with me now. If you were Olivia's darling, you would benefit greatly, but I will keep you away from her to spite her. I will sacrifice a lamb — you, Cesario — to spite Olivia. She has a raven's heart in her dove's body."

Viola revealed her feelings for Orsino: "I, most happily, readily, and willingly, to give you peace and satisfaction, a thousand deaths would die."

"Where are you going, Cesario?" Olivia asked.

"After the man I love more than I love my eyes, more than I love my life, more by far than ever I shall love a wife. If I am lying, then let the gods punish me and take my life for being disloyal to my love."

Olivia said, "I am detested. I have been lied to."

Viola asked, "Who has lied to you? Who has done you wrong?"

"Have you forgotten who you are?" Olivia asked Viola. "Has it been so long?"

She ordered a servant, "Bring the priest to me."

Orsino said to Viola, "Let's go now."

Viola began to move after Orsino, but Olivia said to her, "Where to, my lord? Cesario, my husband, stay here."

"Husband!" Orsino said.

"Yes, husband. Can he deny that we are married?"

Orsino asked Viola, "Are you married to Olivia?"

"No, my lord, not I."

Olivia said to Viola, "It is your base fear that makes you deny that you are married to me. Do not be afraid, Cesario. Reveal your good fortune. Acknowledge that you are my husband, as you know that you are, and then, because Orsino will know you are married to a Countess, you will have nothing to fear from him."

The priest walked toward Olivia, who said to him, "Welcome, father! Please, reverend father, tell everybody — although we had wanted to keep secret what now we must reveal due to circumstances — what you know has recently happened between this young man and me."

The priest said, "You two have made an eternal bond of love. This was confirmed by the mutual joining of your hands, attested by the holy kiss of your lips, and strengthened by the exchange of rings. I as priest and witness sealed all the ceremony of your eternal bond of love. My watch tells me that you two were married two hours ago."

Orsino said to Viola, "You lying little cub of a fox! How evil will you be by the time you have a few grey hairs on your head? Or will you become so evil so quickly that it will trip you and destroy you even before you grow gray? Goodbye. Stay with your wife, but make sure that I never see you again."

Viola replied, "My lord, I swear —"

Olivia interrupted and said, "Do not swear! Keep at least a little faith even though you are afraid of Orsino."

Sir Andrew came running up to the group of people. His head was bleeding a little. He did not see Viola.

He shouted, "For the love of God, get me a doctor and send a doctor to Sir Toby!"

"What's the matter?" Olivia asked.

"He has hit me on the head and has bloodied Sir Toby's head, too! For the love of God, get me some help! I would give more than forty pounds to be safe in my home."

"Who has done this, Sir Andrew?" Olivia asked.

"Orsino's young gentleman. His name is Cesario. We took him for a coward, but he fights like the very Devil incarinate."

Viola thought, *Sir Andrew means "incarnate" or "incarnadine" — blood-red — or both.*

"My gentleman?" Orsino asked. "Cesario?"

Sir Andrew noticed Viola and said, "My God! Here he is! You hit me on the head for nothing. Whatever I did, I did it because Sir Toby wanted me to do it."

"Why are you saying that I hurt you?" Viola said, remembering her earlier "duel" with Sir Andrew. "I never hurt you. You drew your sword upon me without cause, but I spoke to you respectfully, and I did not hurt you."

"If giving someone a bloody head is hurting him, then you have hurt me," Sir Andrew said. "Do you think that a bloody head is nothing?"

Sir Toby came up to them, with Feste assisting him.

Sir Andrew said, "Here comes Sir Toby limping. You shall hear more about the fight. If he had not been drunk, he would have touched you with his sword."

Orsino asked, "What's wrong with you, Sir Toby?"

"Nothing important," Sir Toby answered. "A man has defeated me in a fight, and that is all there is to it."

He asked Feste, "Fool, have you seen Dick the doctor?"

"He is drunk, Sir Toby," Feste said. "He has been drunk for an hour. His eyes were closed because of drunkenness at eight in the morning."

"Then he's a rogue, and he is slow and reeling like someone dancing a passy measures panyn — a slow and stately dance that requires reeling like a drunk from side to side. I hate a drunken rogue."

Olivia said, "Take Sir Toby away and get him help. Who has made this havoc with them?"

Sir Andrew said, "I'll help you, Sir Toby. You and I can have our wounds taken care of together."

Sir Toby was angry because he had lost a fight and been wounded and he was especially angry because Olivia was angry at him. He took out his anger on Sir Andrew: "You will help me? You are an ass and a fool and a knave. You are a thin-faced knave and a sucker!"

Olivia said, "Put Sir Toby to bed, and find someone to take care of his wound."

Feste, Fabian, Sir Toby, and Sir Andrew left.

Sebastian now came running up to Olivia. He did not notice Viola or Antonio.

He said to her, "I am sorry, Olivia, that I have hurt your uncle, but even if he had been my own brother, I would have been forced to hurt him for my own safety."

Olivia was looking strangely at him, for good reason.

He said to her, "You are looking strangely at me, and because of that I know that my action has offended you. Pardon me, sweet one, and remember the vows we made to each other so recently."

Orsino looked back and forth at Sebastian and Viola. He said, "One face, one voice, one style and color of clothing, and two persons. An optical illusion made by nature. It seems to be real, but it can't be!"

Sebastian noticed Antonio. He went to him and said, "My dear Antonio! The hours since I have been separated from you have racked and tortured me since I did not know where you were and whether you were safe."

"Are you Sebastian?" Antonio asked.

"Can you doubt that I am, Antonio?"

"How have you managed to divide and duplicate yourself? An apple, cut in two, is not more alike than you and this other person. Which of you two is Sebastian?"

Olivia said, "This makes me full of wonder."

Seeing Viola, Sebastian said, "Is that me standing there? I never had a brother, and I do not have the powers of a deity — I am not here and everywhere. I am not omnipresent. I had a sister, but she drowned in the remorseless waves and swells of the sea."

He said to Viola, "Be kind and tell me, how are you related to me? We so resemble each other that we must be related. Which town and country are you from? What is your name? Who were your parents?"

Viola replied, "I come from Messaline. Sebastian was my father's name. It was also my brother's name. He drowned and now has a watery tomb. If spirits can take on the appearance and the clothing of the deceased, you have come here to frighten us."

"I have a soul, indeed, but my soul is still clad with the body that I received while I was still in my mother's womb. If you were a woman instead of a man, since everything but that says that you are my sister, I would hug you and let my tears fall upon your cheek, and say to you, 'Welcome, drowned Viola! Welcome, and welcome again!'"

Viola said, "My father had a mole upon his brow."

"And so did my father."

Viola said, "My father died on the day when Viola turned thirteen years old."

"I remember well the day my father died. He did indeed die on the day that my sister turned thirteen years old."

Viola said, "If nothing else prevents our mutual happiness at finding each other except these deceptive male clothes that I have used to disguise myself, do not hug me until each circumstance of place, time, and fortune fit together and prove that I am Viola. To confirm that I am Viola, I will take you to a sea captain in this town. In his house, he has my female clothing. He helped save my life so that I survived to serve Duke Orsino. Ever since the shipwreck, I have served as a messenger between Orsino and Olivia."

Sebastian said to Olivia, "So this is how you mistook me for my sister, whom you did not know to be a woman. But nature corrected that mistake and turned it to your advantage. By loving my sister, you were loving someone like me. If the mistake had not been corrected, you would have married a maiden. Nevertheless, you were not deceived. You have married both a maiden and a man. I am a man, but I am also like a maiden — I am a virgin."

Olivia, of course, was shocked by the discovery that she had married someone whom she had just met.

Orsino said to her, "Don't worry. This young man — Sebastian — is of noble blood. You have not married a commoner."

He added, "If all these things are true, and they seem to be, since Sebastian and Cesario — as I call her — are mirror images of each other, then I also shall benefit from this most fortunate shipwreck."

He said to Viola, "Disguised as a young man, you have said to me a thousand times that you never would love a woman as much as you love me."

"All those sayings I will swear again," Viola said. "They are as true as the fact that the Sun shines on the Earth and separates day from night."

Orsino said to her, "Give me your hand."

They held hands.

He said to her, "Let me see you dressed in your female clothing."

Viola replied, "The captain who brought me safely to shore has my female clothing, but he is now in jail because of a complaint brought against him by Malvolio, who is a gentleman and a servant to Olivia."

Olivia said, "Malvolio shall set the sea captain free."

She ordered a servant, "Go and get him."

Then she said, "But wait. I remember now that people say that he, poor gentleman, has become insane."

Feste and Fabian now walked up to the group of people.

Olivia said, "My own distractions completely made me forget about him."

She asked Feste, "How is Malvolio?"

"He is keeping off Beelzebub as well as a man in his condition may do. I have in my hand a letter that he wrote to you. I should have given it to you this morning, but the letters of a madman are not gospel truth and so it does not matter much when they are delivered."

Olivia ordered, "Open the letter, and read it out loud."

Feste said, "When a fool reads the words of a madman, there is much to be learned."

He imitated the voice of a madman as he read, *"By the Lord, madam —"*

"What are you doing? Why are you reading the letter like that? Are you yourself mad?"

"No," Feste answered, "but I am reading madness. If you want me to read the letter out loud as it ought to be read, you must allow me to read it in the voice of a madman. It must be a dramatic reading."

She told him, "Read it as a man who has his right wits would read it."

"I am doing that," Feste said, "but the right wits of a madman are different from the right wits of a sane man. Therefore, perpend and be attentive, and listen."

For once, Feste had misjudged his audience. Olivia respected Malvolio, and she was angry at Feste.

Olivia told Fabian, "You read the letter out loud."

Feste gave Fabian the letter.

Using his normal voice, but louder, Fabian read, *"By the Lord, madam, you wrong me, and the world shall know it. Although you have put me into a dark room and given your drunken uncle rule over me, yet I have the benefit of my senses as well as your ladyship has. I have your own letter that induced me to act as I did. This letter will justify my actions and show that you have behaved shamefully. Think about me as you please. As your steward, I should be more polite, but I am aggrieved. THE MADLY USED MALVOLIO."*

Even when he thought that he had a grievance against Olivia, Malvolio was conscious of his duty and aware when he was not living up to his own standards.

"Did he write this?" Olivia asked Feste.

"Yes, madam."

Orsino said, "This letter does not sound as if it were written by a madman."

Olivia ordered, "Fabian, release Malvolio from the dark room and bring him here."

He left to go and get Malvolio.

Olivia said to Orsino, "My lord, I hope that after you think these things over that you will like to have me as a sister-in-law instead of as a wife. If you agree, on the same day two weddings will be held that will make us in-laws. We will have the weddings here at my house and at my expense."

Orsino replied, "I am happy to accept your offer."

He said to Viola, "I release you from having to do service to me. Because you have done me service for so long, which was unfeminine and beneath your soft and tender breeding, and since you have called me master for so long, here is my hand."

Viola held it.

Orsino continued, "You shall be my wife."

Olivia said, "And you shall be my sister-in-law!"

Fabian arrived, leading Malvolio.

Orsino asked, "Is this the supposed madman?"

"Yes, my lord," Olivia replied. "This is he."

She asked, "How are you, Malvolio? What has happened?"

He replied, "Madam, you have done me wrong — outrageous wrong."

"Have I, Malvolio?" Olivia said. "No."

"Lady, you have. Please, read this letter I have."

He handed it to Olivia, who began reading it.

"You cannot possibly deny that this is your handwriting. Try to write differently from it, in handwriting or in choice of words. Try to say that this is not the seal with which you stamp your letters. Try to say that this is not your style. You cannot deny any of these things. Therefore, admit that you wrote that letter and explain honestly and sincerely to me why you wrote so clearly that I was in your favor, why you wrote that I should smile and put on cross-gartered yellow stockings, why you wrote that I should frown upon Sir Toby and people lower in social status than I am, and why, after I obediently followed all your instructions and hoped for your love, you allowed me to be locked in a dark prison, visited by the priest, and made the most notorious fool and sucker who was ever tricked. Tell me why."

"I am sorry, Malvolio," Olivia said, "but this is not my handwriting, although I confess that it is much like my own. But unquestionably this is Maria's handwriting. And now I remember that it was Maria who first told me that you were mad. Afterward, you came in smiling and you were dressed in such a way and you acted in such ways that this letter told you to do. Please, do not be so upset. This practical joke badly fooled you, but when we know the motivations and the perpetrators of this joke, you will be the plaintiff and the judge in your own case. You will pass judgment and give any sentences."

Fabian, who did not want Olivia angry at him, said to her, "Good madam, hear me speak, and let no quarrel or brawl spoil the pleasure of this present hour and the planning of two marriages, which has amazed me. In hope that present pleasure shall not be ruined, very freely I confess that I and Toby set up this practical joke to make a fool of Malvolio because we have seen some arrogant and discourteous qualities in him. Maria wrote the letter at Sir Toby's great insistence. Because of that, he has married her. How the practical joke played out with entertaining mischievousness should lead to laughter rather than revenge if we consider the injuries that both sides — Malvolio and us — have endured."

Not only had Malvolio been made a fool, but now he had to listen to Fabian say that the practical joke was justified and something that should cause laughter.

Olivia said to Malvolio, "Poor fellow, how have they exposed you to ridicule!"

Feste said to Malvolio, "Why, 'Some are born great, some achieve greatness, and some have greatness thrown upon them.' I was one, sir, in this interlude; I was one Sir Topas, sir; but that doesn't matter. 'By the Lord, fool, I am not mad.' But do you remember what you said earlier? 'I marvel that your ladyship takes delight in such an uninspired rascal. Unless you laugh and encourage him to make jokes, he is gagged and unable to say anything.' The wheel of fortune turns and brings revenge."

Malvolio said calmly and coldly to Fabian, "I'll be revenged —"

Fabian's face fell.

Malvolio turned and faced Feste and finished, "— on the whole pack of you."

Feste's face fell.

Angry but unbroken, Malvolio then bowed to Olivia and went inside her house.

Olivia had not been impressed by Fabian's and Feste's words. She said, "Malvolio has been most outrageously abused." She made it clear that she was angry.

Orsino said to a couple of his servants, "Pursue him and entreat him to make peace."

Olivia shook her head at Orsino. Malvolio needed to be alone for a while.

Orsino raised his hand in a Stop gesture, and the servants who had started to go after Malvolio stopped.

Olivia thought, *It is better to talk to Malvolio after he has recovered somewhat from his ordeal.*

Orsino said to Olivia, "Malvolio has not told us about the sea captain yet. When we have learned that part of the story and when the proper time has come, we shall hold our two weddings. In the meantime, sweet sister-in-law, we will stay here and talk."

He added, "Cesario, come; for so I shall call you while you are dressed as a man. When you dress in female clothing and are seen, then you will be my wife and my Queen."

Everyone went into Olivia's house except for Feste, who was once again in trouble with Olivia and who sang this song:

"When that I was only a little tiny boy,

"With hey, ho, the wind and the rain,

"A foolish thing was but a toy,

"For the rain it raineth every day.

"But when I came to man's estate,

"With hey, ho, the wind and the rain,

"'Gainst knaves and thieves men shut their gate,

"For the rain it raineth every day.

"But when I came — alas! — to take a wife,

"With hey, ho, the wind and the rain,

"By swaggering could I never thrive,

"For the rain it raineth every day.

"But when I came unto my beds,

"With hey, ho, the wind and the rain,

"With toss-pots [sots] still had drunken heads,
"For the rain it raineth every day.
"A great while ago the world was begun,
"With hey, ho, the wind and the rain,
"But that's all one, our story is done,
"And we'll strive to please you every day."

And such is life for many fools. We are born, become children, and have mischievous deeds dismissed as trifles, and then we reach maturity and go from underachievement to underachievement. Possible opportunities disappear and both important and "important" people often shut their gates against us because they think that we are knaves or thieves, and we often grow to regret either having a spouse or not having a spouse. After boasting to ourselves about the great things we will do, we often find ourselves not able to do them. We grow older, we find that life grows tougher, we have thoughts that keep us awake at night, and the preferred entertainment of many people, perhaps including ourselves, is getting drunk. Our stories are just some more such stories of very many such stories in the history of the world. As with fools, so with Malvolio — and you and me.

Appendix A: Who is the Proudest and Most Evil Character in Twelfth Night?

Note: This brief essay includes but enlarges on some material found above in my retelling of the play.

When Maria writes a letter to fool Malvolio into making an ass of himself, she includes the letters M, O, A, I. Malvolio realizes that this is a puzzle, and he tries to solve the puzzle. He believes that the letters refer to himself because all of the letters are in his name.

Malvolio did not correctly solve the puzzle of M, O, A, I. True enough. But what is the correct solution to the puzzle? What if M, O, A, and I are — in part — an anagram? We certainly have seen Malvolio and the people spying on him when he finds the letter in Olivia's garden talk about rearranging the letters. Malvolio tells us that A should go after M, and Fabian mentions O and end. What do we get when we rearrange the letters and put I at the beginning? I M A O. I am A and O. The O goes at the end, and the end is Omega. If the end is Omega, what is the beginning? The beginning is Alpha. Therefore, I am Alpha and Omega. This is Revelation 22:13 (King James Bible): "*I am Alpha and Omega, the beginning and the end, the first and the last.*" These are words — and letters — that apply to God, but Malvolio is applying them to himself. Revelation is the last book of the Bible. What is the first book of the Bible? Genesis. What is the most important part of Genesis? The Fall. The serpent tempted Eve to eat the fruit of the Tree of Knowledge of Good and Evil: "*For God doth know that in the day ye eat thereof, then your eyes shall be opened, and ye shall be as gods, knowing good and evil*" (Genesis 3:5, King James Bible). Eve — and Adam — ate the fruit, committing the sin of pride. They placed themselves before God and disobeyed the command of God. The sin of pride is regarding oneself as the center of the universe, as being more important than anything or anybody else. Pride is a deadly sin, and it is the foundation of the other deadly sins:

1) Pride.

I am the center of the universe, and I am better than other people. Quite simply, I am more important than other people.

2) Envy.

I am the center of the universe, so I ought to have it all, and if you have something I want, I envy you.

3) Wrath.

Because I am the center of the universe, everything ought to go my way, and when it does not, I get angry.

4) Sloth.

I am the center of the universe, so I don't have to work at something. Either other people can do my work for me, or they can give me credit for work I have not done because if I had done the work, I would have done it excellently.

5) Avariciousness and Prodigality.

I am the center of the universe, so I deserve to have what I want. If I want money, I get money and never spend it, or if I want the things that money can buy, then I spend every dime I can make or borrow to get what I want. Either way, I deserve to have what I want.

6) Gluttony.

I am the center of the universe, so I deserve these two extra pieces of pie every night. This is my reward to myself for being so fabulous.

7) Lust.

I am the center of the universe, so my needs take precedence over the needs of everyone else. If I want to get laid, it's OK if I lie to get someone in bed and never call in the days and weeks afterward. My sexual pleasure is more important than the hurt of someone who realizes that he or she has been used.

Malvolio's name is Mal Volio — "I wish badly." Proud people wish badly.

The rebellion of Adam and Eve in the Garden of Eden led to the first sin committed by human beings. Previously, an angel had committed the first sin by supernatural beings.

That proud supernatural being is Lucifer, who put himself before God and rebelled against him. Because of this sin, Lucifer is condemned to spend eternity shackled in the darkness of Hell. Adam and Eve committed the original sin of human beings. Lucifer committed the original sin of supernatural beings.

If Malvolio were a better person, he would solve the puzzle of I M A O correctly and he would realize that he is guilty of the sin of pride. He wants to marry Olivia, but he wants to marry her because doing so will improve his position in society. He does not want to marry Olivia because he can make her happy. He loves Olivia's social standing and her wealth.

Malvolio regards himself as being more important than Olivia: I am the center of the universe, and I ought to marry Olivia because doing so will make ME happy. I am the center of the universe, and I ought to marry Olivia for her social standing and money. I am the center of the universe, and I ought to marry Olivia although I do not love her.

If Malvolio were a more intelligent person, he would realize that he on the verge of a fall just like Adam and Eve were when the serpent tempted them in the Garden of Eden or like Lucifer when he rebelled against God.

Malvolio is not morally good enough or intelligent enough to correctly solve Maria's puzzle, and he believes the letter that Maria wrote and he will be punished for believing it just like Lucifer was punished. However, the people judging him and punishing him are not God.

There are important differences in Malvolio's sin and the sin of Adam and Eve and of Lucifer:

1) Adam and Eve actually ate the fruit of the Tree of Knowledge of Good and Evil, and Lucifer actually led a rebellion of some angels against God. Malvolio wants to marry Olivia although he does not love her — he does respect her — because it will improve his social status. However, he does not actually marry Olivia. Motive is important in judging, but so are consequences.

2) God judges Adam and Eve and Lucifer. Who judges Malvolio? Mainly Maria and Sir Toby. We do have evidence that Malvolio is proud from Olivia, who tries to make peace between Malvolio and Feste after Malvolio criticizes Feste after he returns from a long absence. She tells Malvolio that he is "sick of [from] self-love." But Olivia is not judging Malvolio in order to punish him. She is trying to make peace between Malvolio and Feste.

3) God judges sinners, and God punishes them. God gives people free will, and he judges them after they die and then either rewards or punishes them. If a sinful human being repents before dying, even with his or her last breath, that person will be rewarded with Paradise. Maria and Sir Toby judge Malvolio and punish him by treating him as if he were insane.

Maria writes M, O, A, I in her letter, but to whom do those letters most apply? Malvolio, or Maria? They apply to Maria more than they apply to Malvolio.

Maria thinks this: I am the center of the universe, and therefore I can judge and sentence Malvolio however I see fit. I am greater than God because I am able to judge Malvolio now instead of giving him a chance to repent before his death.

As I see it, Maria and Sir Toby are the most evil characters in the play. What punishment do they sentence Malvolio to undergo? They sentence Malvolio to be bound and placed in a room that is as dark as Hell. (In actual performance, the binding (at least of hands) apparently does not take place, as we know because Malvolio is able to write a letter to Olivia. Also, it allows actors more freedom of movement.) How is Lucifer punished? He is bound and placed in Hell, which is in eternal darkness. Only God can justly judge a person and justly give such a punishment.

Maria is the person most responsible for judging Malvolio. Sir Toby participates in the fooling of Malvolio, but he lacks a good brain. Maria is more intelligent than Sir Toby, who is more intelligent than Sir Andrew, who allows himself to be manipulated by Sir Toby. Fabian and Feste play roles in the fooling of Malvolio, but they at least admit to Olivia the roles that they played. Their 'confessions' are problematic, however, as Fabian wants to avoid getting in trouble with Olivia and Feste states that one reason for him to be involved in the practical joke is revenge for the time that Malvolio criticized him in front of Olivia.

What is Malvolio's real sin?

Malvolio's sin is wanting to marry Olivia although his reason is to advance his social standing — we have no indication that Malvolio feels romantic love for her. (Malvolio also thanks Jove, not God, for what he thinks is his good fortune. Wanting to marry someone simply in order to improve one's social standing is unChristian.)

Some of Malvolio's "sins" are not sins. Sir Toby is angry at Malvolio for wanting to stop the late-night party, but Malvolio works for Olivia and his job as steward is to help run the household and to carry out her orders, which include trying to keep Sir Toby from partying — his partying keeps her from sleeping. Sir Toby shows pride because he thinks that a mere servant such as Malvolio ought not to tell him — a knight! — not to party so much.

Malvolio also lacks diplomacy. He criticizes Feste in front of Olivia. If he were more intelligent, he would realize that Olivia enjoys Feste's foolery and therefore Feste is providing good value for his room and board and whatever stipend he may get.

Malvolio appears to be a very competent steward and may be a bit of a workaholic. He walks in Olivia's garden, which ought to be a source of pleasure and entertainment, but he does such things as practice his courtly gestures, something that would make him a better steward.

Many of Malvolio's faults are not sins. We think that Feste is a fine fool and that Malvolio is missing out by not appreciating his foolery. We think that there is a time for work and a time for play, but Malvolio appears not to take much time to play — the most fun he has in the play is imagining what he would do if he and Olivia were married. One thing that he would do is to rebuke Sir Toby — if anyone ever needed to be rebuked, that person is Sir Toby.

When it comes to fun, everyone needs to have some fun, but the amount that is appropriate varies with age. Young children should spend most of their free time playing. College students should spend a lot of time studying but still have time for fun. Older people such as Malvolio — and Sir Toby — definitely should have fun, but they should also be productive. For workers such as Malvolio, chances are that they have little time for fun. Sir Toby basically sponges off his niece and suckers such as Sir Andrew; he contributes little to anyone. Feste's job is providing fun for others, and that is a difficult job indeed.

Can a person judge whether another person is really having fun? You may attend a play that you enjoy. You notice a critic who is not laughing with the audience, but who is watching the play intently. You think that the play will receive a mediocre review at best, but the next day you read the critic's review and find out that he or she was having the time of his or her life. (My idea of a good time is sitting on the couch and reading a good book — Sir Toby would probably walk in on me and ask, "Where are the cakes and ale?")

One fault that Malvolio has is an inability to appreciate satire. That is one reason he criticizes Feste. If an inability to appreciate good and real satire — some so-called "satire" is not satire — were a sin, however, many people we consider to be good would go to Hell.

Malvolio does show one sin — understandably — at the end of the play: anger. He vows to get revenge "on the whole pack of you." We are not told to whom he says it, but my guess is to Fabian and Feste, who have confessed their part in the cruel practical joke but who have not expressed remorse for what they did — remorse is an important part of religious confession. Malvolio's anger is a direct result of the cruel practical joke and its aftermath. By thinking up and performing the practical joke, Maria has given Malvolio an opportunity to sin. We are horrified that Lady Macbeth leads her husband to sin. Maria's sin is not as bad as that of Lady Macbeth's because a steward, even if he were to turn evil, cannot cause as much damage as a Thane or a King.

Malvolio has sinned in his desire to marry Olivia simply in order to improve his social standing — we have no evidence that he loves Olivia. He does not repent that sin. We can note that Lucifer also does not repent his sin. None of the sinners in Dante's *Inferno* repent. But Malvolio is not yet dead, and he has time to repent.

Anyone who sees *Twelfth Night* thinks that Malvolio is treated way too harshly for whatever faults he has. Shakespeare understood human nature, and he had to have known that this is the way that we would feel. Therefore, this is the feeling that he wanted us to have: He wanted us to sympathize with Malvolio. Usually, Malvolio is seen as the bad guy in the play, but I think that, despite Malvolio's faults, Sir Toby and Maria are much more evil than Malvolio, with Maria being the most evil — and the proudest — of all.

Perhaps actors are not playing Malvolio correctly if they cry and scream when Malvolio is locked in the dark room. Perhaps he maintains his dignity while he is in the dark room. If he did, that would prevent the cringing that the audience feels when the actor playing Malvolio cries and suffers. Audiences, in my opinion, should feel sympathy for Malvolio when he is imprisoned, but they should not cringe. (When the actor playing Malvolio cries and screams, I feel that the actor is saying, "Hey, everybody! Look at me! I'm acting!") And although Malvolio is angry, perhaps when he says at the end of the play that he will be revenged on "the whole pack of you," perhaps he says that only to Feste and Fabian — the other members of the pack are Sir Toby and Maria, who are not present. Perhaps he says this calmly and coldly and not furiously. His anger may be a controlled anger. What happens to Malvolio after the end of the play? We don't know, but one possibility is that he goes to his room in Olivia's house, freshens up, and then tries to decide on the proper punishments for those who mistreated him. Olivia told him that he would be prosecutor and judge. No doubt he found them guilty and as judge he must decide on the proper punishments: ones that are severe enough to satisfy him but not so severe that Olivia changes her mind about letting him be judge.

By the way, in Dante's *Inferno*, we find out what is at the center of the universe. Dante believed that the Earth was at the center of the universe. The Inferno, aka Hell, goes all the way down to the center of the Earth, which is where Lucifer is imprisoned. Dante and his guide, Virgil, need to travel up to the Earth's surface on the other side of the entrance of Hell so that they can reach the Island of Purgatory, so they climb down Lucifer's body to reach a passageway leading to Purgatory. At Lucifer's midpoint, they turn around and reverse direction because they have reached the center of the Earth and are no longer going down but are heading up again. What is the exact center of the universe? It is located in Lucifer's rectum.

One final point: All of sin is based on pride, and all of us have sinned. All of us have at one time or another considered ourselves to be the center of the universe.

Recommended Reading

Inge Leimberg, "'M.O.A.I.' Trying to Share the Joke in *Twelfth Night* 2.5 (A Critical Hypothesis)." *Connotations* 1.1 (1991): 78-95.

Appendix B: About the Author

It was a dark and stormy night. Suddenly a cry rang out, and on a hot summer night in 1954, Josephine, wife of Carl Bruce, gave birth to a boy — me. Unfortunately, this young married couple allowed Reuben Saturday, Josephine's brother, to name their first-born. Reuben, aka "The Joker," decided that Bruce was a nice name, so he decided to name me Bruce Bruce. I have gone by my middle name — David — ever since.

Being named Bruce David Bruce hasn't been all bad. Bank tellers remember me very quickly, so I don't often have to show an ID. It can be fun in charades, also. When I was a counselor as a teenager at Camp Echoing Hills in Warsaw, Ohio, a fellow counselor gave the signs for "sounds like" and "two words," then she pointed to a bruise on her leg twice. Bruise Bruise? Oh yeah, Bruce Bruce is the answer!

Uncle Reuben, by the way, gave me a haircut when I was in kindergarten. He cut my hair short and shaved a small bald spot on the back of my head. My mother wouldn't let me go to school until the bald spot grew out again.

Of all my brothers and sisters (six in all), I am the only transplant to Athens, Ohio. I was born in Newark, Ohio, and have lived all around Southeastern Ohio. However, I moved to Athens to go to Ohio University and have never left.

At Ohio U, I never could make up my mind whether to major in English or Philosophy, so I got a bachelor's degree with a double major in both areas, then I added a master's degree in English and a master's degree in Philosophy.

Currently, and for a long time to come (I eat fruits and vegetables), I am spending my retirement writing books such as *Nadia Comaneci: Perfect 10*, *The Funniest People in Dance*, *Homer's* Iliad: *A Retelling in Prose*, and *William Shakespeare's* Macbeth: *A Retelling in Prose*.

By the way, my sister Brenda Kennedy writes romances such as *A New Beginning* and *Shattered Dreams*.

Appendix C: Some Books by David Bruce

Retellings of a Classic Work of Literature

Arden of Faversham: *A Retelling*

Ben Jonson's The Alchemist: *A Retelling*

Ben Jonson's The Arraignment, or Poetaster: *A Retelling*

Ben Jonson's Bartholomew Fair: *A Retelling*

Ben Jonson's The Case is Altered: *A Retelling*

Ben Jonson's Catiline's Conspiracy: *A Retelling*

Ben Jonson's The Devil is an Ass: *A Retelling*

Ben Jonson's Epicene: *A Retelling*

Ben Jonson's Every Man in His Humor: *A Retelling*

Ben Jonson's Every Man Out of His Humor: *A Retelling*

Ben Jonson's The Fountain of Self-Love, or Cynthia's Revels: *A Retelling*

Ben Jonson's The Magnetic Lady, or Humors Reconciled: *A Retelling*

Ben Jonson's The New Inn, or The Light Heart: *A Retelling*

Ben Jonson's Sejanus' Fall: *A Retelling*

Ben Jonson's The Staple of News: *A Retelling*

Ben Jonson's A Tale of a Tub: *A Retelling*

Ben Jonson's Volpone, or the Fox: *A Retelling*

Christopher Marlowe's Complete Plays: Retellings

Christopher Marlowe's Dido, Queen of Carthage: *A Retelling*

Christopher Marlowe's Doctor Faustus: *Retellings of the 1604 A-Text and of the 1616 B-Text*

Christopher Marlowe's Edward II: *A Retelling*

Christopher Marlowe's The Massacre at Paris: *A Retelling*

Christopher Marlowe's The Rich Jew of Malta: *A Retelling*

Christopher Marlowe's Tamburlaine, Parts 1 and 2: *Retellings*

Dante's Divine Comedy: *A Retelling in Prose*

Dante's Inferno: *A Retelling in Prose*

Dante's Purgatory: *A Retelling in Prose*

Dante's Paradise: *A Retelling in Prose*

The Famous Victories of Henry V: *A Retelling*

From the Iliad *to the* Odyssey: *A Retelling in Prose of Quintus of Smyrna's* Posthomerica

George Chapman, Ben Jonson, and John Marston's Eastward Ho! *A Retelling*

George Peele's The Arraignment of Paris: *A Retelling*

George Peele's The Battle of Alcazar: *A Retelling*

George Peele's David and Bathsheba, and the Tragedy of Absalom: *A Retelling*

George Peele's Edward I: *A Retelling*

George Peele's The Old Wives' Tale: *A Retelling*

George-a-Greene: *A Retelling*

The History of King Leir: *A Retelling*

Homer's Iliad: *A Retelling in Prose*

Homer's Odyssey: *A Retelling in Prose*

J.W. Gent.'s The Valiant Scot: *A Retelling*

Jason and the Argonauts: A Retelling in Prose of Apollonius of Rhodes' Argonautica

John Ford: Eight Plays Translated into Modern English

John Ford's The Broken Heart: *A Retelling*

John Ford's The Fancies, Chaste and Noble: *A Retelling*

John Ford's The Lady's Trial: *A Retelling*

John Ford's The Lover's Melancholy: *A Retelling*

John Ford's Love's Sacrifice: *A Retelling*

John Ford's Perkin Warbeck: *A Retelling*

John Ford's The Queen: *A Retelling*

John Ford's 'Tis Pity She's a Whore: *A Retelling*

John Lyly's Campaspe: *A Retelling*

John Lyly's Endymion, The Man in the Moon: *A Retelling*

John Lyly's Galatea: *A Retelling*

John Lyly's Love's Metamorphosis: *A Retelling*

John Lyly's Midas: *A Retelling*

John Lyly's Mother Bombie: *A Retelling*

John Lyly's Sappho and Phao: *A Retelling*

John Lyly's The Woman in the Moon: *A Retelling*

John Webster's The White Devil: *A Retelling*

King Edward III: *A Retelling*

Mankind: *A Medieval Morality Play* (A Retelling)

Margaret Cavendish's The Unnatural Tragedy: *A Retelling*

The Merry Devil of Edmonton: *A Retelling*

The Summoning of Everyman: *A Medieval Morality Play* (A Retelling)

Robert Greene's Friar Bacon and Friar Bungay: *A Retelling*

The Taming of a Shrew: *A Retelling*

Tarlton's Jests: A Retelling

Thomas Middleton's A Chaste Maid in Cheapside: *A Retelling*

Thomas Middleton's Women Beware Women: *A Retelling*

Thomas Middleton and Thomas Dekker's The Roaring Girl: *A Retelling*

Thomas Middleton and William Rowley's The Changeling: *A Retelling*

The Trojan War and Its Aftermath: Four Ancient Epic Poems

Virgil's Aeneid: *A Retelling in Prose*

William Shakespeare's 5 Late Romances: Retellings in Prose

William Shakespeare's 10 Histories: Retellings in Prose

William Shakespeare's 11 Tragedies: Retellings in Prose

William Shakespeare's 12 Comedies: Retellings in Prose

William Shakespeare's 38 Plays: Retellings in Prose

William Shakespeare's 1 Henry IV, aka Henry IV, Part 1: *A Retelling in Prose*

William Shakespeare's 2 Henry IV, aka Henry IV, Part 2: *A Retelling in Prose*

William Shakespeare's 1 Henry VI, aka Henry VI, Part 1: *A Retelling in Prose*

William Shakespeare's 2 Henry VI, aka Henry VI, Part 2: *A Retelling in Prose*

William Shakespeare's 3 Henry VI, aka Henry VI, Part 3: *A Retelling in Prose*

William Shakespeare's All's Well that Ends Well: *A Retelling in Prose*

William Shakespeare's Antony and Cleopatra: *A Retelling in Prose*

William Shakespeare's As You Like It: *A Retelling in Prose*

William Shakespeare's The Comedy of Errors: *A Retelling in Prose*

William Shakespeare's Coriolanus: *A Retelling in Prose*

William Shakespeare's Cymbeline: *A Retelling in Prose*

William Shakespeare's Hamlet: *A Retelling in Prose*

William Shakespeare's Henry V: *A Retelling in Prose*

William Shakespeare's Henry VIII: *A Retelling in Prose*

William Shakespeare's Julius Caesar: *A Retelling in Prose*

William Shakespeare's King John: *A Retelling in Prose*

William Shakespeare's King Lear: *A Retelling in Prose*

William Shakespeare's Love's Labor's Lost: *A Retelling in Prose*

William Shakespeare's Macbeth: *A Retelling in Prose*

William Shakespeare's Measure for Measure: *A Retelling in Prose*

William Shakespeare's The Merchant of Venice: *A Retelling in Prose*

William Shakespeare's The Merry Wives of Windsor: *A Retelling in Prose*

William Shakespeare's A Midsummer Night's Dream: *A Retelling in Prose*

William Shakespeare's Much Ado About Nothing: *A Retelling in Prose*

William Shakespeare's Othello: *A Retelling in Prose*

William Shakespeare's Pericles, Prince of Tyre: *A Retelling in Prose*

William Shakespeare's Richard II: *A Retelling in Prose*

William Shakespeare's Richard III: *A Retelling in Prose*

William Shakespeare's Romeo and Juliet: *A Retelling in Prose*

William Shakespeare's The Taming of the Shrew: *A Retelling in Prose*

William Shakespeare's The Tempest: *A Retelling in Prose*

William Shakespeare's Timon of Athens: *A Retelling in Prose*

William Shakespeare's Titus Andronicus: *A Retelling in Prose*

William Shakespeare's Troilus and Cressida: *A Retelling in Prose*

William Shakespeare's Twelfth Night: *A Retelling in Prose*

William Shakespeare's The Two Gentlemen of Verona: *A Retelling in Prose*

William Shakespeare's The Two Noble Kinsmen: *A Retelling in Prose*

William Shakespeare's The Winter's Tale: *A Retelling in Prose*